MW01265117

Jungle Blaze

Shifting Desires Series, Volume 3

Lexy Timms

Published by Dark Shadow Publishing, 2018.

This is a work of fiction. Similarities to real people, places, or events are entirely coincidental.

JUNGLE BLAZE

First edition. May 27, 2018.

Written by Lexy Timms.

Also by Lexy Timms

A Chance at Forever Series
Forever Perfect
Forever Desired
Forever Together

BBW Romance Series
Capturing Her Beauty
Pursuing Her Dreams
Tracing Her Curves

Beating the Biker Series
Making Her His
Making the Break
Making of Them

Billionaire Holiday Romance Series
Driving Home for Christmas
The Valentine Getaway

Cruising Love

Billionaire in Disguise Series
Facade
Illusion
Charade

Billionaire Secrets Series
The Secret
Freedom
Courage
Trust
Impulse

Building Billions
Building Billions - Part 1
Building Billions - Part 2
Building Billions - Part 3

Conquering Warrior Series
Ruthless

Diamond in the Rough Anthology
Billionaire Rock

Billionaire Rock - part 2

Dominating PA Series
Her Personal Assistant - Part 1
Her Personal Assistant Box Set

Fake Billionaire Series
Faking It
Temporary CEO
Caught in the Act
Never Tell A Lie
Fake Christmas

Firehouse Romance Series
Caught in Flames
Burning With Desire
Craving the Heat
Firehouse Romance Complete Collection

Fortune Riders MC Series
Billionaire Biker
Billionaire Ransom
Billionaire Misery

The Boss
The Boss Too
Who's the Boss Now
Love the Boss
I Do the Boss
Wife to the Boss
Employed by the Boss
Brother to the Boss
Senior Advisor to the Boss
Forever the Boss
Christmas With the Boss
Gift for the Boss - Novella 3.5

Model Mayhem Series
Shameless

Moment in Time
Highlander's Bride
Victorian Bride
Modern Day Bride
A Royal Bride
Forever the Bride

Outside the Octagon
Submit

The Boss
The Boss Too
Who's the Boss Now
Love the Boss
I Do the Boss
Wife to the Boss
Employed by the Boss
Brother to the Boss
Senior Advisor to the Boss
Forever the Boss
Christmas With the Boss
Gift for the Boss - Novella 3.5

Model Mayhem Series
Shameless

Moment in Time
Highlander's Bride
Victorian Bride
Modern Day Bride
A Royal Bride
Forever the Bride

Outside the Octagon
Submit

Celtic Mann
Heart of the Battle Series Box Set

Heistdom Series
Master Thief

Just About Series
About Love
About Truth
About Forever

Justice Series
Seeking Justice
Finding Justice
Chasing Justice
Pursuing Justice
Justice - Complete Series

Love You Series
Love Life
Need Love
My Love

Managing the Bosses Series

Reverse Harem Series
Primals
Archaic
Unitary

RIP Series
Track the Ripper
Hunt the Ripper
Pursue the Ripper

R&S Rich and Single Series
Alex Reid
Parker

Saving Forever
Saving Forever - Part 1
Saving Forever - Part 2
Saving Forever - Part 3
Saving Forever - Part 4
Saving Forever - Part 5
Saving Forever - Part 6
Saving Forever Part 7
Saving Forever - Part 8
Saving Forever Boxset Books #1-3

Battle Lines

The Brush Of Love Series
Every Night
Every Day
Every Time
Every Way
Every Touch

The Debt
The Debt: Part 1 - Damn Horse
The Debt: Complete Collection

The University of Gatica Series
The Recruiting Trip
Faster
Higher
Stronger
Dominate
No Rush
University of Gatica - The Complete Series

T.N.T. Series
Troubled Nate Thomas - Part 1
Troubled Nate Thomas - Part 2
Troubled Nate Thomas - Part 3

Wash
Loving Charity
Summer Lovin'
Love & College
Billionaire Heart
First Love
Frisky and Fun Romance Box Collection
Managing the Bosses Box Set #1-3

JUNGLE BLAZE

Shifting Desires Book # 3
By Lexy Timms
Copyright 2018

Jungle Blaze

Shifting Desires Book #3

Cover by: Book Cover by Design[1]

Shifting Desires Series

Book 1: Jungle Heat
Book 2: Jungle Fever
Book 3: Jungle Blaze

Find Lexy Timms:

LEXY TIMMS NEWSLETTER:
http://eepurl.com/9i0vD
Lexy Timms Facebook Page:
https://www.facebook.com/SavingForever
Lexy Timms Website:
http://www.lexytimms.com

Want to read more...
For **FREE**?
Sign up for Lexy Timms' newsletter
She'll keep you updated on her new releases, fun giveaways, free reads
and other great stuff! You can unsubscribe at any time you want
Sign up for news and updates!
http://eepurl.com/9i0vD

JUNGLE BLAZE BLURB:

ANGELICA HAS TAKEN the jungle home this time.

After traveling to two different jungles on two different continents, you'd think she would be done with exotic locales for a while. But the lion inside isn't easily controlled, and now she needs help from the wisest elders in the shifter community.

The last thing Taylor wants to do is risk Angelica in the wildest jungle on the planet, but he's got no choice. His own government has betrayed him, and a woman from the past is hot on their... tails?

From the wilds of Minnesota to the highest mountains in Nepal, Angelica and Taylor are on the run one last time. The adventure isn't over by a long shot, and time is running out if they're going to meld the woman to the beast within.

Chapter 1

Angelica tossed and turned. She'd woken him up again. Taylor lay there a moment, still groggy and trying to get his bearings, but knew she wasn't doing well. His hand shot out to steady her, to pull her back within the circle of his arms. He murmured soft things, stroking her shoulder, her hair, until she stilled and her breathing evened out. He hated this, hated the helpless feeling of not being able to save her from the nightmares. She still hadn't let go of having to shoot Dr. Johns. It haunted her every night, tearing her from sleep somewhere after midnight with a consistency that created a new normal. It left a bad taste in his mouth whenever he thought about it. He pressed his lips to her hair, and listened to the sounds of the city traffic that filtered up to his apartment from the street below.

He'd thought things would be better here. Angelica had had enough of jungles and, to be honest, so had he. They came back to D.C. for an extended rest, to figure out next steps, but that was a big order. Trying to fit a normal life into one that recently included being shot at would be enough to make readjustment difficult. But add being kidnapped and experimented on to it, and that would give anyone a good sized dose of PTSD.

He wondered what word one would give to the trauma that came of suddenly being able to shift into a large predator. Especially when one hadn't grown up expecting the change to happen, right alongside all the other readjustments that happened at puberty.

It's going to take time to handle. A lot of time.

In the meantime, she had nightmares and he lost sleep. They both were losing sleep.

"*Shh,*" he whispered when she whimpered again. He held her and stroked her head, willing her to leave the dream a second time; this time for good, that she might get some rest for once. And by extension allow him the same luxury.

She'd told him it was always the same dream, a memory really, of children being hurt, of her firing a gun at Melinda. Melinda's body falling and the blood everywhere. He understood those dreams because he'd had them, too. The difference was, he was trained as a CIA agent. Angelica's training was medical. Everything she believed in went against the taking of lives.

Even if taking Melinda's life meant saving his.

He, at least, had received a certain amount of training on how to deal with these situations. He was given counseling as part of his de-briefing. While his memories were no less pleasant, he was taught how to deal with the necessity of sometimes having to take lives.

She had been wholly unprepared for it. And what's worse, given the outcome of the entire fiasco, she hadn't been able to seek counseling to help her over the rough edges.

He wrapped his arm around her and murmured soothing words against her hair, words that meant nothing in themselves, but carried with them the comfort and surety he could give them. It was a balm, an absolution. It was a nightly ritual.

One of them.

It was the other that was most troubling.

In the short time they had been back in D.C., they'd spent a fortune on bedding. They'd replaced the mattress twice. He'd lost count of the sheets and blankets they'd gone through, and it had only been a month since they'd gotten back.

It was easier when I went through this. But I was going through puberty back then. They prepared us for it. We slept on large pillows until we could prove we could go a full night without destroying the furniture.

According to his mom, it was like bathroom training all over again. As a child you learn to recognize the signs of a full bladder, the same way you learn as a teen what it feels like to change into a white tiger in your sleep. Well, in Angelica's case she became a golden-brown lioness, but the same ideas held true.

She stilled. It was only a matter of time now.

Taylor listened for the crack of bone, the grinding of flesh that was the sound of the change. They slept naked, a rule not just from the effect of lovemaking from two people in love and betrothed to each other, but clothing was restrictive and could cause injury during a change.

But that didn't mean a displaced claw didn't catch the sheets and shred them, or tear open a mattress. She'd started joking about water beds, but he could tell she was scared. She didn't seem to have any control over the change.

Whereas his was natural and he'd grown into it, hers was forced on her. Their time in Africa had been disastrous. While she'd discovered a previously unknown tribe of shifters who became lions, she'd been captured by the mad doctor desperate to study them. So desperate, in fact, that she'd been working on creating them artificially. It had been Taylor's fault that Angelica had gotten tangled up in the whole mess. If he hadn't been a shifter himself, she never would have believed what she was seeing. She might have stayed safe. They might not have captured her and done things that never should have been able to work to her.

But I'd never heard of anyone altering DNA to create a shifter before.

And now here she was with no training, no preparation of her mind for the things her body was going through. There was no way for her to combat a spontaneous change.

And it was getting worse.

He stroked her hair and kissed her cheek. He held her close and told her it was all right, that whatever had plagued her was over. It was a lie, but it served to calm her. He partially woke her to get her to rest again. Then he fell back and covered his face with an arm. She would be moaning and twitching again in an hour, he knew it. She wouldn't get deep sleep, and by extension neither would he.

He wondered for a moment what it would be like if he still had to go to work, still had be the agent he'd trained to be, with no sleep. His concentration was already off. He was supposed to show up at the office sometime in the afternoon. How many hours away was that now? He'd taken all the vacation time he'd had, and Randall had been getting impatient with him. But how could he explain?

In the meantime, his own inner cat was calling to him to change, to run and explore and hunt. In an apartment complex in D.C.

Was it a mistake to come here?

But it was home, such as it was. There was only so much wilderness within range, and the last thing he needed was tales of big cats roaming the Appalachian Trail. Especially one that was unable to practice deception, to hide the fact that she was a big cat, or about to change into one. So taking her out of the city was impossible. But trying to keep her in it was worse.

Not that it was her fault. She had little control over that. Without him there to monitor it, she would change and leap out an open window before she realized where she was, or even what she was. She'd woken up several times as a cat, always in a tree or stalking a barking dog on the other side of a fence. She never hurt one, she never would. He suspected it was the hunt she wanted. But every time she suddenly realized where she was, she had to try to figure out how to get home again. Sometimes, that wasn't easy. Especially since this city was still fairly new to her.

And each time she changed increased the risk that someone would see her and report a fully-grown lioness running loose. This time, she was calmed. This time, she fell asleep next to him, her soft skin touching his, her chest rising and falling, her long, lovely legs spread over the mattress in blissful slumber.

An hour from now, she might be tearing the sheets as her body broke and reformed. Or two. Or three. Or not at all. Taylor tried to sleep around that, nodded off when his body demanded it, when it screamed for a little rest. The times when he pushed too hard, stayed up too often, those were the times he ended up outside in his bathrobe, hunting a lioness with a glass of water. Splashing her face was the best bet he had to startle her awake.

For the moment, he lay in the darkness, staring at the ceiling and breathing the foul city air. It was a nice change from the clean, muggy breath of the Amazon rainforest or the cloying jungles of Africa. Here, there were millions of people getting on with their lives and not one of them was hunting him or Angelica. Here, the greatest danger was the expressway during rush hour. Here in the polluted skies, no one knew where they were.

Should have killed the bad one when you had the chance.

He sighed. That was new. What changes Angelica was going through overwhelmed him, but he was trying to save her and deal with his own issues stemming from Melinda's interference. She'd forced him to change at her will, had experimented on him—the only test subjects she'd had were lions, so he was the first white tiger she'd seen... and she had been curious.

But before Melinda, he and the cat never interacted. The cat called him the "other memory", a small voice that consoled caution and helped the cat stay under the radar of man; for his part, Taylor was human without any real memory of when he was a tiger. But that had all changed. Now it was like sharing a brain with another person. Correction, it *was* sharing a brain with another person. The cat spoke to him now. That was a lot to deal with and, frankly, he was never sure he wasn't just going crazy.

We did kill her.

No, the fat one.

That was the name the cat gave Griselda. She was a large, round woman who looked like someone's futzy grandmother. She also ran one of the world's most intricate drug cartels. She'd seen him change. She'd been the financial backing behind Melinda. She was still alive.

I can't just kill for no reason... yes, I now see that there was a reason. But at the time I had no idea that she was going to be a part of our lives forever.

The cat didn't respond. Taylor got the feeling he was sulking.

You don't kill without cause, either, he reminded the cat. He sighed in the silence of his mind and found himself drifting off. He jerked awake and lifted his head to study his love. She slept soundly. He lay back down and closed his eyes.

It was barely moments before he was awake. Very awake.

"ANGELICA!" he screamed, and clapped his hands.

She jerked awake and gasped. She turned and looked at him. He could see her realize that her body was shifting. She closed her eyes and concentrated, the hair receded from her legs, and her hands smoothed out again into long elegant fingers.

"I'm sorry." She sounded tired. Defeated. "Did you get any sleep at all?"

He rolled over and wrapped an arm around her. "Let's try again," he said. He even sounded exhausted to himself.

Chapter 2

"Hello?" Taylor wondered if he sounded as raw as he felt. Of course, it was rude of whomever it was to call at... well, it was after 9:00. All good little agents should be up by now anyway. The problem wasn't being up, the problem was *still* being up.

"Don't come in to work. Not today. Not tomorrow."

Taylor blinked. He'd been trained and had a great deal of experience thinking fast on his feet, it was a hazard of the profession, but he was still asleep, or still not asleep...

"Randall?"

"A certain military man has been asking questions about you and the good doctor. Leading questions. Regarding the late Dr. John's experiments."

Taylor was suddenly, dreadfully, awake. The breath caught in his throat and he tried to think what he needed to ask first. There were too many questions to sort through. He went with the obvious. "I thought that was buried."

"It was." Randall's tone was apologetic. A touch angry. "And sealed. This is something else—I don't know where this came from, but the military applications..." He left the rest unsaid.

Maybe it wasn't the first time that it occurred to someone that an army full of soldiers who could flow over the battlefield in a formation of tigers and could instantly heal non-fatal wounds would be a great benefit. But it was a first coming from his own government. He glanced at Angelica as she shifted, stretched sleepily. Suddenly she seemed too vulnerable, too close to, well, everything. The District of Columbia wasn't the best place to be right now.

"How bad is it?" Taylor asked, not wanting to hear the answer.

Angelica sat up and looked at him, eyes still full of sleep. Of concern. He reached for her, taking her hand in his.

"Bad." Randall's voice was low. He spoke rapidly. "They're looking into *your* security clearance. *Your* background."

It took him a minute to catch the emphasis. If they were looking into his background that meant his history, his family. What was it Dr. John said? Something about studying his people? Had she written something down? Said something to someone about the idea? He thought of the sleepy little community he'd grown up in. They'd fled to America long ago to escape this kind of notice.

"You told me this was taken care of, that there wouldn't be any repercussions." His voice was sharp. It wasn't fair to blame Randall. He'd been a friend as well as a boss, and had violated a dozen or so internal regulations to protect Taylor's secret, but the chill that had hold of his guts wasn't being rational let alone fair. If that footage of his change, if any notes of who and what he was, still existed then Taylor had endangered his own family, not to mention his community. Whatever came next would be on his head. And for better or worse, Randall was the bearer of the news.

They were against me leaving the community in the first place for this very reason. I asked them to trust me. I promised them this wouldn't happen.

"This didn't come from my office." Randall hissed. "And you know the footage we captured in Africa was accidently destroyed." There was a slight pause. "I made sure of it personally."

Taylor gathered his thoughts. Make that a couple dozen internal regulations and a few federal laws that his friend had violated for Taylor's sake. For Angelica's sake. He pinched the bridge of his nose and sighed. "Look... I..."

"Yeah, I know," Randall said. "It's okay—I freaked out a little, too."

By this point Angelica was mouthing questions, trying to figure out what was going on. Taylor shook his head, motioning for her to wait.

She sighed a little and flopped back against the pillow. Bits of stuffing flew in all directions. It hadn't been a good night for bedding.

Don't get distracted. Focus.

He returned his attention to Randall. "Can you find out where this came from?"

"I'm working on it, but it happened somewhere in the inner workings of the Pentagon, completely bypassing the normal network."

"That's telling all by itself," Taylor thought out loud and rubbed his forehead. "So, whoever it was, they had full access to someone with a lot of brass." There weren't too many people on that particular list.

"That's the way it looks."

"Someone connected to the slave ring?"

Angelica's head shot up. Her eyes took on a frightened look.

Although Dr. Johns had denied knowledge of it her research was, at least in part, funded by a human trafficking operation run from a refugee camp. When Taylor and Angelica busted up the operation, at least one very prominent American general disappeared and hadn't been seen since. The repercussions were still being felt.

"It's an angle we're perusing." Randall's voice was strained. Taylor could match the look that went with it: the pursed mouth, the frown etching heavy lines into his forehead. Worried, Randall looked like a man in severe need of a digestive aid.

"I'm sorry," Taylor sighed. "I know you are... I...I need to call home, I guess."

"Yeah. That would be a good idea." Randall paused for a moment and added, "Probably not from this phone. For that matter, I'd be very careful about what you do or say for a time." He thought for a minute. "Tell you what: you two need a good vacation, a chance to rest up from all your hard work in Africa, so why don't you go home, let Angelica meet the folks, take a little time, just the two of you."

"Thanks, but..." Taylor shook his head. There was too much to do and taking Angelica anywhere until her training was done was risky.

She could very well turn in front of someone. The idea of her losing control on an airplane was terrifying. Of course, most of the problems they'd been having were because he'd been the one to change in front of someone. Becoming a white tiger in front of the head of a drug cartel, for example. He was about to ask Randall if they'd pursued that particular lead, when Randall added a little gem to think about.

"I'll make it official," he said. "I'll call it an investigation and put your lady on as a consultant."

Taylor looked at the phone in his hand. It was a very generous offer. If going back to Minnesota was 'official' business, then all the expenses around it were paid. Airfare, hotel, car rental, all of it.

It's not like any of this is his fault. But he's not taking it well. Like this is personal. He's feeling bad that the information got out.

"That's... thank you," Taylor said and looked up at Angelica, who was about to burst from curiosity. The way her muscles were twitching it was all she could to not lean over and plaster her ear against the phone to find out what was going on. That she was respecting his space was amazing and wonderful and one of the reasons he loved her. He smiled, and reached out to touch her cheek. "I'll think about it, okay? Let me see how the call goes and figure it out from there."

"All right, but let me know. I'll come up with a charge code, just let me know what you need," Randall said, then added quickly. "Within reason."

"Private jets are very reasonable," Taylor pointed out with a grin.

"Glad to see you're feeling better." Randall snorted and hung up.

Angelica was on him the second he dropped the phone back on the nightstand. "What was that all about?" she asked, wrapping herself around him and looking very seriously into his eyes.

I don't want to tell her.

She was too eager, too interested. Too... her. Bright and beautiful and everything he'd ever dreamed. And he was about to destroy her world. She'd been so good about the change so far, dealing with the frustration of the uncontrolled transformations with a certain aplomb, even if it scared her. And he knew it did. Her body was completely out of her control at this point, yet so far she'd never once given in to the fear. Not only that, she was having to rely on him to get her through the night. For someone as independent as Angelica, it was a hard transition to let go and allow someone else to take care of her, when she was the one used to doing all the caregiving.

"Taylor?"

Her expression became guarded. Uncertain.

"Someone in the Pentagon found out about us," he said finally.

I want to give her the reassurance that everything would be all right. But right now he didn't have enough information to do that. And he refused to lie to her.

She froze. Expressionless. She didn't speak. He wasn't sure she could. He could see her mind working, the implications coming on her faster than she could take it in.

"How?" It was barely a whisper.

"Randall's trying to figure that out. I don't know. But…" He took a breath and then took her hand, holding it tight. "In order to join the CIA… hell, in order to get clearance while still in the Marines, they had to do an extensive background check on me." He could see that it didn't register with her and so he elaborated.

"People—military people—had to go out and interview my parents. All my relatives."

"Okay, I still don't follow," Angelica said. "To work with Doctors International they talked to my mom, too."

Taylor licked his lips. "Remember what Melinda said? She said that I opened 'another supply of test subjects', she just needed to do some research into my background."

"Melinda is dead," Angelica said, and dark shutters fell over her eyes. "She was unbalanced, disturbed."

He was losing her, back into the morass of her dreams. He took her chin in his hand, forcing her to lift her head and look at him.

"You can't go there right now. I need you to listen to me. Okay?"

She nodded.

"You think there aren't people in the Pentagon just as disturbed as she was? Hell, these are the same people who used LSD on people without their knowledge, who sprayed DDT on children in swimming pools."

"But..." Angelica was trying to understand. "They can't just take an entire town—"

"You mean like Melinda did?"

"But this is America—things like that don't happen here!"

"Yes," Taylor looked into her eyes so she would understand him. "Yes, they do. And with alarming frequency."

She seemed smaller suddenly. More fragile. Damn, he hated doing this to her.

"So, what do we do?" She might have been scared out of her mind, but he loved her for asking. *That's my girl. Don't let fear keep you down.*

"We?" Taylor echoed, and smiled. "*You* need to continue your exercises. Don't moan, you have to control this..."

"But they're not working," Angelica protested, rising to the bait. "And I feel stupid."

"It's how we're trained," Taylor insisted, glad he could give her something to focus on. To take the sting out of the news she'd just gotten.

Angelica dropped her head to her chest. "Fine," she said with all the enthusiasm of a rebellious teen. She sat up. "And what are you going to do?"

"I think this is a really good time to call home," Taylor said and dug in the drawer for a new burner phone. Maybe he was being paranoid, but Randall was right. He would have to be cautious from here on out.

He found one and rummaged around for a sim card to fit. "Let's just hope they'll think the same when I tell them."

Angelica left him to it and padded into the bathroom. Taylor watched her go. She was a beautiful woman, dark curls cascading down her back. He eyed her trim waist, that beautiful backside, and for a moment wanted nothing more than to call her back to the bed where they could do their best to forget the world and all its dangers for an hour. She glanced back at him once, eyeing him with brilliant eyes, and smiled when she saw that his body was reacting to what he'd been looking at. She twitched her hips playfully and shut the bathroom door.

He fell back against the pillows and sighed.

Back to the matter at hand.

Minutes loaded, he dialed a number he'd not used in a long time but would never forget. "Hey, Dad..."

Chapter 3

D ulles had been the stuff nightmares were made of. It took a very
long time for them to get to the plane and past security. Taylor
had overnighted a package to himself—care of his parents' farm in
Minnesota. Still, unarmed and even wearing slip-on loafers to get past
security made him feel distinctly vulnerable, despite the fact that he
could call upon the tiger if things went south. Right now he trusted no
one—except for Angelica.

*But you won't. The tiger is there, but the last thing you need right now
is to show it to anyone.*

It was a lie, but one he needed to tell himself right now. If her life
was in danger he wouldn't hesitate to protect her. The tiger thrummed
just beneath the surface, agreeing with quiet vehemence.

Damn the torpedoes, full speed ahead.

They were told to report to a gate, and then the flight was changed
to another gate at the other end of a very long terminal. They ended
up running to make it in time. No one even apologized. They were giv-
en coach tickets, though he'd paid business class, and he was forced to
shoehorn his 6'5"-frame into a seat made for someone Angelica's size.
His knees rubbed the seat in front of him and the tray table wouldn't
lie flat. Then the guy in that seat reclined and Taylor let out a howl of
pain.

"Maybe we don't fly this airline anymore," Angelica said, holding
his hand.

"Is there an airline called 'Separated'? That's what I want to fly right
now." His fingers curled around hers until she grimaced. "Sorry." He
loosened his grip. Marginally. He knew that he was grouchy, it was late
nights and stress, but this flight wasn't helping.

He ordered coffee once they were airborne. As luck would have it they were out. He asked for a 7-Up and the waitress blithely dropped a Sierra Mist on the tray table she tried to force flat over his aching knees in unwanted helpfulness. He pulled himself up in the seat in self-defense so he could straighten his legs and save his kneecaps from further damage.

"Please remain in your seat, sir!" The airline hostess was positively seething at this point, somehow managing to put her frustration on him, as though it was his fault the seat had been sized for midgets.

"Taylor..." Angelica leaned over to pat his arm. "Take a breath. You have all day before your report to the FAA—you can manage." She managed to somehow convey that she was confiding in him, while at the same time pitching her voice to make sure it carried.

The hostess did a classic double-take and her artificial smile seemed to be screwed on tighter. "Can I get you anything else, sir?" she asked, all sweetness and light.

"No," Taylor said with just as much saccharine. "I have everything I need."

"Yes, sir," she said, and moved on to the next passenger.

"Club soda?" Angelica asked the woman's retreating figure.

It was almost impossible not to laugh at how quickly the woman's back stiffened, or how quickly that club soda appeared.

The rest of the flight was thankfully unremarkable, though it took him a good five minutes to untie his legs from the seat. He stretched and heard a distinctive popping sound that really shouldn't have been there.

"Yeah." He looked down at Angelica, whose face reflected equal parts horror and concern. "I'm changing tickets for the trip back. Any airline but that one. Or we drive."

If Dulles was a warren to get through, the airport in Minneapolis was under construction. This was a perpetual state with this particular airport. Apparently they started on one end, worked to the other, and started over again. If he ever flew in and there weren't plastic tarps surrounded by workmen somewhere, he'd think he was in the wrong place.

They made two wrong turns before getting to the car rental counter. The girl behind the desk didn't look old enough to drive, much less work there. She checked her records, *tsk*ing through a mouth filled with braces, and frowned, her eyes becoming lost under her shaggy black hair cut to hide her from the world, which seemed at odds with the multiple face piercings designed to draw attention.

"I'm sorry, sir, but we're out of mid-sized cars at the moment. I can get you a sub-compact..." She looked up at him, took in his shoulders and height and said, "Well, maybe not. I do have a pickup truck I can substitute for no extra charge; it's quite nice, and brand new."

Taylor snorted. "That's going to make us blend in with the natives." He shot a look at Angelica, who was snickering, and agreed to the change.

Gathering their bags, they found the rental truck and tossed the luggage in the back. It was a warm, clear day—Minnesota summer at its best. They headed out to his rural roots, stopping for a decent lunch. It was a relief to sit in a seat meant for someone his size.

"Do your exercises," he reminded her as he drove.

"I can't!" Angelica protested, shoving her hair off her sweaty forehead. "They don't work. I keep telling you that."

"It's how—"

"Maybe it's how you learned to control it, how everyone learns to control it. I get that, but it isn't working for me. Maybe I'm just too stupid to figure out how to be a shifter, but it's not working!" They drove for a while in silence. "This isn't the way to cure me!" she muttered finally. He could see her out of the corner of his eye, staring at her hands clasped in her lap as though they would change at any minute.

"It's not a disease," Taylor said after a moment.

"Then why are you treating it like one? Taylor, I'm a doctor, I know about physical therapy, I know about exercise. These are not working for me. I'm sorry if I don't 'get it', but I don't."

"That's what we're here for!" Taylor snapped. He even sounded petty to himself. "Like I said before, I only know what it's like for me. I don't have the tools or training to look into your DNA. Maybe someone back home will know. I don't know. They've been doing this for hundreds of years. Maybe they can determine what's wrong. What with the way it was forced on you... I don't think there's ever been an artificial shifter before." He let that trail off. It was old ground they'd covered extensively before they'd left on this journey.

"Artificial? Excuse me?"

He winced. This too was becoming a sore spot between them. "Well... man-made, then. All the training for this was created for natural shifters."

They drove in silence for a while. Taylor fumed. The fact was, she *was* artificially created as a shifter, she *did* have the ability forced on her from someone cutting her DNA to match another's, and the sooner she accepted that the sooner she would be able to use the techniques to control her shifts.

Only, she stubbornly refused to listen.

"You sure you didn't just drag me here to meet your folks?" she asked after a moment. He looked away from the road long enough to see the hesitant smile on her face. He had to give her credit for this, for making the effort to meet him halfway.

He smiled back. *Okay, so truce then.* "Well, not *just* for that." He looked at her for a moment and took a guess. "Is that what you're worried about? Meeting my family?"

"Well—" She shrugged, but the tension didn't leave her shoulders. "It's about equal, really." She held up fingers. "On one hand, there's changing into a lion unexpectedly and painfully." She held up the other hand. "And then there's meeting your parents." She balanced them, the second hand suddenly heavier.

"Well, of course they'll love you," he assured her then hesitated, his natural honesty leading him to tell the rest. "Eventually."

"Uh... eventually?"

"Look, the... we don't often bring in non-changers. It's awkward and it can be dangerous. The fact that you're a lion and not a tiger will be... unexpected. I had no idea there was a variety of changers. I've never met any outside of my family group." He waved that off. "But non-changers aren't all that uncommon, really. If we stuck to our own, we'd be inbred." He held up a hand. "Don't say it."

"I wasn't going to say anything at all," she said sweetly, batting her eyelashes at him dramatically.

"You're really not all that good at that innocent thing, you know that, right?"

Angelica stuck her tongue out at him. It was a good thing he was driving; he could pretend not to notice. "Yeah, I admit that I'm nervous about the whole meet the parents thing. The other I can deal with if I have to. At least I haven't changed in public."

"Not yet," Taylor reminded her ominously. "But it's close enough that it could happen."

"That's a cheery thought."

"You *did* get outside more than once," he reminded her, "and had to change back once I caught you. That was very much in public. It's just a good thing the complex doesn't have security cameras or there would be animal control prowling the streets."

"Yeah." She nodded slowly. "I don't really want to change back and find I'm naked in a cage in a zoo."

"You need to check your posture," he reprimanded her. "Stand and sit straight."

"'Be as human as I can in thought and carriage,'" she said, repeating the words he'd been drilling into her since she'd become a lion the first time.

"I know, I know, but it's important. At least till we get someplace safe."

"So why did we stop to eat if I'm such a risk?"

"Because I was hungry," he snapped, finishing the last of the roast beef sandwich he'd had nestled in his lap, untouched for the past five miles. "And you'll note we didn't eat in the restaurant." Angelica winced. "Besides, it's a long drive yet. We've got a couple hours on the road."

"I think I might take a nap for a while if you don't mind."

"That's fine." Taylor nodded and wadded up the wrapping the sandwich had been in and threw it back into the bag. "You can do your exercises later. Considering it's a pickup, it's actually kind of comfortable. If you can wait until we pull off, you can rearrange yourself to your heart's content."

Not many miles further on they came to a coffee shop. Taylor bought a large coffee for the road, then shifted the suitcases out of the cab and stashed them in the bed of the truck. There was a small area behind the seats. It was meant for passengers, judging from the padded seats and seatbelts, but when someone Taylor's size drove, he had to have his seat all but touching that one. He'd joked that it was reminiscent of the plane trip in and shuddered at the memory.

Angelica found a teddy bear for sale at the register and picked it up for a makeshift pillow. "At least we haven't run into werebears yet," she said under her breath and he reached over and rapped the shelf twice with his knuckles. Back in the cab she reclined her seat all the way and curled up to nap.

The tires sang on the highway in a way that only new rubber does. The truck was new, the chassis was tight, and driving was a pleasure.

Taylor put in ear buds and cranked the ZZ Top collection on his phone as they headed down the highway.

He'd been watching the road, his ears blocked by 'Sharp Dressed Man', and didn't notice the napping lioness beside him for quite a few miles. He nearly drove off the road when the tail came and slapped him in the middle of his forehead.

"So much for not changing in public," he mused, staring at her shredded clothing. Change hurt. Change meant breaking bones, organs shuffled and compressed. Change while being dressed meant strangulation and restriction. It was actually moderately dangerous, depending on what one was wearing at the time.

She'd slept through all of it.

What was worse was the realization that he needed to wake the lioness.

In a very, *very* confined space.

Chapter 4

She woke and knew instantly she'd shifted. Her yellow eyes glanced at the large man in the small space beside her. She growled, not at him but at the fact she'd gone and done it. Now she was hungry.

Focus.

She closed her eyes and let herself shift back, trying to ignore the pain and hoping her claws hadn't wrecked the rental.

Taylor had new clothes in his hand. A simple slip-on dress that she'd packed in her carry-on. Lucky he'd tossed it at her before they left. She put it on and stared out the window as Taylor sighed and shifted the truck back into drive.

It was better just to stay awake. Awake, she could straighten her back and think of being a person. No, more than think about it. She needed to *focus* on being a person. This was the first exercise. The problem was, trying to not think about something was like that old joke where you tell a child to *NOT* think of a purple gorilla. Once the idea is planted, it's all the child can think of. So here Angelica was to *not* think of being a lioness.

Only, once triggered, the change was always just on the edge of happening.

Fighting it was a moment by moment battle. One that was both taxing and draining.

This is how he learned. This is how they all learned, apparently. Why can I not get this? What is it that I'm missing?

It was more than frustrating; it was dangerous. It was also true that she had been outside as the lioness and that she had been lucky not to have been spotted. He'd been right to point out that the apartment complex could easily have had security cameras. Or what if someone had been outside at the time? People walked dogs. Or came home from work. Or one of a multitude of reasons that would have them driving around in the middle of the night. She'd been damn lucky, and it was time she realized that.

I know I'm getting snappish. I just... I wish we could talk about something else for a change. He used to say, "I love you", and now it's, "Do your exercises." Is there a possibility that he resents me being able to shift, too? It's not like I'm trying to take away his uniqueness. But I didn't exactly volunteer for this!

Then there was the other battle. The one she tried to avoid mentioning to Taylor. The one where she woke in the middle of the night, every night, lying in the darkness listening to Taylor breathing, seeing Melinda in her mind's eye as the woman's body jerked and fell under the rain of bullets from Angelica's gun.

If she hadn't shot, Taylor would be dead. Melinda had already put one bullet in his shoulder. If she had been any better of a shot, she would have put it where changing wouldn't have helped. Angelica had been in the position of being forced to choose between what had been hardwired into the very fabric of her own personal belief system, and the man she loved. Maybe she was naïve. She'd certainly been accused of it before. But it had seemed, and still did seem, wrong to take life from another human being despite who they were or what they did.

Now it haunted her dreams. It haunted her waking hours, too. It was an image that would be burned in her mind forever. Someone's ability to become a better person, to make a positive impact on the world, had been stripped from them.

And you also took away her ability to do evil—which is exactly what she had been doing. You did the right thing. You did the only thing you could. How many people had she already killed in her experiments? How many more people would need to die before it would have been okay to kill her?

She was a doctor; killing was an anathema, a slap to everything she believed in. And so the debate still raged.

Maybe the hardest thing to confront was her own conviction that, in order to save his life, she would do it all over again. That was what kept her awake, what stuck in her mind like a burr she couldn't dislodge.

And she couldn't even talk about it.

She'd come to him about it once, trying to make him understand her own mixed feelings and the problems she was having, and all he did was remind her that she'd done what she'd had to; she'd killed to save him. The idea that *she'd killed* he hadn't seemed to understand. He had absolutely no idea how much of a hole that single act had burned into her soul.

"Do your exercises," he reminded her as the scenery passed by in a blur.

FUCK my exercises.

Angelica held her arm up in front of her, as if she were concentrating on it, and instead found herself staring at the scenery as though the answers would be written on the thick pine forest just beyond her window. She longed for the chats, the talks that passed the time on long trips, the comradery of laughter and the intimacy of sharing the sights. Not that they'd been carefree when they'd left the jungle in South America together, but there had never been this terrible silence between them. And the trip she'd taken with him before leaving for Africa had been… well, they'd only had a rushed weekend on the coast, at a little resort so, long travel time hadn't happened. But even there, everything had been… well, fresh and new. They'd spent ages in finding out the little details, favorite colors and movies, and whether he liked Thai food better than Mexican.

Now, when they had all this time on the road, the only thing they seemed to talk about involved lions. Or tigers.

She picked up her stuffed bear and tacked on the 'oh my' just to be facetious.

She traded one arm for the other while he tapped the steering wheel and half sang under his breath about a Mexican Blackbird.

When was the last time we talked about anything else? Really talked?
She let the bear drop into her lap.

When was the last time we played?

Even the sex had become an opportunity for a fucking lesson. Angelica snorted. Right now, she wouldn't mind a "fucking" lesson. The last time he'd taken her he had her worked up, her juices flowed, her heart sang, and she was squirming in the most delicious way. And just as he parted her sex with his and began to enter her, he told her to keep her humanity in mind.

It was a glass of ice water on her passion. Just at the moment he entered her, she lost all desire to be touched because it was just *ANOTHER FUCKING LESSON.*

Angelica put her arm down and looked at him. The earphones were still firmly in place and he was lost between ZZ Top and the road. Angelica stared at the teddy bear, thinking that he was fast becoming the better conversationalist. And was cozier for snuggling up to in bed.

Be fair. You bitch about him not considering your feelings, but what about his?

He looked like he was interested in the music, in the road trip, but there was a crease in his forehead that hadn't been there before Randall had called, and it hadn't left since.

He's worried about his people.

It was a small distinction, but shouldn't that be 'our' people? If not because she was a shifter, too, then just because they were a couple and because his family would... might... be hers someday? Or was it all none of her business because...

She didn't want to finish the thought. Right now, everything felt too much like it was falling apart. Sadly, the bear held no answers for her, nor could he do anything to change anything. She tucked him under her arm and watched the trees whip past the window.

"Taking a break?"

Angelica smiled and reminded herself for the thousandth time that he was just trying to help her. "Yeah." She nodded, not really looking at him.

"Well, that's okay," he said, pulling out the ear buds. "I know you don't like them, but they're important exercises, you know?"

"Yes. I understand." She took a steadying breath. "So, do you think your folks are..."

She didn't know how to put the thoughts into words. Not without offending him. Lately all she'd done was offend him.

"I mean, do you think they'll run? Move, I mean?" She glanced over at him, tilting her head to see his eyes, which narrowed a little as he thought.

"'Run' is probably the right way to put it, but don't say that word around my father unless you're talking about a horse. These people don't run from anything." He tried to smile, but instead he just looked sad. "I hope so, I really do. But they've been there a long time."

"You know that none of this is your fault, right? That being found out, that's not because of you."

He acknowledged the comment with a slight nod, but didn't reply.

"Taylor?"

"I shifted in front of her," he said without looking at her. His concentration on the road was fierce, and certainly didn't merit the attention. It was a bright, sunny afternoon, the road was straight, and they had only seen a half-dozen cars in the last hour. "I was so sure that I could... that she wouldn't..."

"She *forced* you to change," Angelica grabbed his arm, wanting him to listen to her. To really listen. If this was what was bothering him. "That pheromone spray—"

"Not her," Taylor said and shot her a look. "Griselda."

She sat back, her hand dropping to her lap.

Oh. *That* her.

Suddenly chilled, Angelica stared at the air conditioning controls as though that were to blame for the way her hair stood up on the back of her neck. "I thought Randall said that..."

"Randall said," Taylor spoke over her, "that it was too soon to figure, but he was looking into it."

"You couldn't have helped that." Angelica tried reaching for him again, but he shook her off.

"I was too pissed. I wasn't thinking straight. I did it just because I wanted to see fear on her ugly face. After everything she'd done to so many people, I just wanted to see her blanch and stammer and wet herself in..." He choked off the rest of what he was going to say. "Because she hurt you," he finished, his eyes still steadfastly on the road.

It wasn't fair. She couldn't accuse him of not letting her help him, or of not paying attention to her words. He could use the excuse of driving to distance himself from the emotions that all this was bringing up. To distance himself from her. Angelica sighed and bit her lower lip.

Just talk to him. Tell him that you miss him, that it doesn't have to be so...

But the moment had passed. The truck slowed, and Taylor signaled to make a turn. "We're here."

The timing was terrible. Angelica had finally worked up the courage to say something. She snapped her mouth shut and looked.

The woods of Northern Minnesota are packed close together, and great grasses and weeds filled in the gaps between the boles. It gave the impression of a solid wall of green, thick and impressive as any medieval fortress. The wall looked unbroken on both sides of the narrow road, as it had for the past fifteen minutes which was about where they'd left the main road.

Unerringly, Taylor turned the truck in to a hole in the wall Angelica didn't even see until they were almost on top of it. He took it slow, but the ruts and holes were still very impressive and the truck bounced and rocked. Angelica braced herself by holding on to a handle over the door and realized suddenly that that was exactly why it was there.

Once he pierced the edge of the wood, the rutted cow path became a road again. The further in he went the better maintained the road became, until they were back on pavement, on a road wide enough for two trucks to pass comfortably.

She had the oddest sensation, like she was Alice just passing through the looking glass.

"Are *you* nervous about seeing your parents again?" Angelica asked. It finally occurred to her that he'd been away for a long time. It might be that part of his churlishness was... fear? It was an interesting thought: the man who took out an entire drug cartel and broke up a slave trade ring was scared of meeting his parents again.

Angelica thought of her mother and let herself feel grateful that she had no such fears. On the other hand, she hadn't just betrayed her mother's biggest secret to someone who wanted to dissect her.

Taylor either hadn't heard her or was ignoring the question. Angelica let it go. It was just another inch separating them, and considering the gap already in place it didn't seem to make much difference anymore.

A dog barked and she turned to see a golden lab mix running after the truck, tail in the air like the periscope on a submarine, running flat out.

A long field to the right showed horses in the distance who frolicked and took off, running a few steps, feeling the warmth on their backs and the open pasture under them.

Taylor drove up to a three-story farmhouse that she hadn't even noticed until now, so intent was she on the scenery It was white with blue trim and looked like it came out of a Norman Rockwell painting, and could have been used for a *Farm Fresh Good to Your Table* advertisement. It was a little too much like the one in *Field of Dreams*, and for a moment she wondered if this had all been a set-up. Or had she just gotten engaged to Opie, and Sheriff Taylor was waiting somewhere just around the corner.

On the porch a man in jeans and blue shirt stood smoking a cigar. He watched the truck snake up the drive and casually reached behind him for a shotgun. She wondered if that might be Taylor's father. Then he took it and aimed it loosely at the cab of the truck, and she hoped that it wasn't just by virtue of the fact that he was so terrifying.

"Taylor," Angelica said, her eyes fixed on the barrel of the gun, "maybe you should tell him who you are."

"He knows," Taylor said glumly as the truck drew even with the porch. "That's why he's got the gun,"

Chapter 5

"I told you I was coming," Taylor said, climbing out of the truck. "And I told you not to bother." While the man wasn't exactly aiming the gun, he wasn't putting it down either. Angelica decided to wait in the truck.

"Harold Mann! You put that down this instant." A tall, rather statuesque woman came out of the house and stood for a moment, arms akimbo, a scowl on her face. Finally, when no one seemed inclined to back down, she walked around him and stood between the two men, facing down the shotgun as though it weren't there at all. "I said put that damn fool thing away."

The shotgun lowered, and after a long moment he replaced it behind him, leaning it against the wall. He threw himself into a large two-person swing hanging from the crossbeam on the porch. His arms were crossed, and even from here Angelica sat could see him seething.

Harold Mann. Taylor's father? No...

Now that she got a look at his face and could see something besides the barrel of the gun, it occurred to her that he was a young man, younger than Taylor, but built around the same lines. The woman turned and hurried off the porch and came to greet Taylor.

She moved like a dancer and had the erect bearing of an aristocrat. Angelica guessed her age at late forties and assumed it was Taylor's mother. *So, the one with gun was expressing some sort of sibling rivalry? What have I gotten myself into?*

Mother and son embraced and Angelica got out of the truck cautiously, keeping a wary eye on the one called Harold. That shotgun was still within easy reach.

"Mother, this is Angelica."

Taylor's mother turned swiftly. Gracefully. Her face split in a wide smile. She came to Angelica with her arms open. She caught her up in hug that nearly took the breath out of her. "Welcome, my dear!"

Angelica thought 'gushing' was too crude a word for a lady like this. She didn't gush, she was... exuberant. For all the stereotypical farmhouse and farmer's wife, she seemed sophisticated in her mannerisms and in how she carried herself, as if pretending the current role.

"Please," Mrs. Mann said brightly, "come in, come in!"

Angelica hesitated perhaps longer than polite. But no matter how much she tried to get her feet to carry her in that direction, they just didn't want to take her there. Maybe she'd faced down too many bad guys already but she'd had enough guns pointed at her to last her lifetime, and wasn't keen on repeating the experience.

Mrs. Mann looked from Angelica to the porch and sighed, clearly exasperated. "Oh, pay him no attention—it's an old argument," She waved off the homicidal Harold as if he were of no importance.

I sure am not going in there alone...

Angelica caught Taylor's hand. "Should we get the bags?" she asked through gritted teeth, dying for a moment alone where she could beg maybe for a ride to the nearest town. Or airport. She didn't belong here. And obviously wasn't welcome.

"Not yet," he said, never taking his eyes off Harold. "Not yet."

Either he wasn't getting her signal to talk, or he did and wasn't about to give her the opportunity. On the up side of things, at least he wasn't exactly clamoring to move back in.

I'm not happy about this.

It wasn't that she was a coward. It was the fact she was going where she was clearly not wanted by at least one person, and was being welcomed with a cautious, if distant warmth by the other. It would have been nice to have Taylor's support, but once again he was so wrapped up in his own thoughts she might as well have been walking up to the house alone.

"Your father is gathering up the council," Taylor's mother announced as she gestured for them to be seated in a very pleasant living room. The furniture was heavy, made of wood, with a thick fabric upholstery over it. Furniture that could endure use by large cats if necessary, she realized. The décor had no fragile knick-knacks, though there was an abundance of art on the walls. Photographs that were portraits of people in bright colors, candid shots warred for space with black and white pictures of ancestors who wore heavy clothing and had faces that showed a grim resolve. Paintings of street scenes from around the world hung next to folk art. In all it gave the room an eclectic, homey feel. Angelica imagined it in the winter, with a fire in the fireplace, and being able to sit curled on that massive couch with one of the books tucked into the long low bookcase that ran underneath the window.

It looked like a good place to grow up. And not what she expected for Taylor at all, given the sparseness of his own apartment.

Taylor's mother bustled in with a platter of cakes from the kitchen, and a pitcher of lemonade alongside a pot of coffee. "They'll all want to hear this, I suspect. I'm not sure if I should ask you to speak, or have you wait until everyone gets here. I'm positively dying of curiosity myself." Her eyes rested on Angelica as she said this.

Angelica blushed and stared at her hands. "Council?"

Taylor's mother smiled. "Town council. If what you said is true, it's something everyone needs to hear. Can I offer you coffee? Or maybe you'd like something cold?" She motioned to the tray.

"Coffee's fine," Angelica murmured, thankful for the distraction.

"Of course it's true," Harold said, slouching against the door that led to the kitchen. "He would know all about it, wouldn't he? He's the fucking cause of it."

"HAROLD!" Taylor's mother snapped. "You will *not* use that kind of language in this house. Profanity is for the weak of mind and for fools who cannot express themselves intelligently."

"Whatever I have to say," Taylor said, pointedly not looking at Harold; instead, busying himself with a slice of cake, "I will say to the full council and let them decide." He lifted his fork, using it to point at what Angelica assumed was his brother. "Not you."

"I already decided," Harold said, taking a step into the room fists balled.

"ENOUGH!" Taylor's mother jumped to her feet, physically putting herself between them the way she had outside. "Both of you."

"I apologize," Taylor said rather stiffly, "but I will not get sucked into a useless conversation, only to have to repeat it all over again when cooler heads arrive."

Harold glared at him for a long moment and spun on one heel, heading out the front door and slamming it hard behind him.

Not exactly the happiest of families, is it?

"Angelica?"

She turned to see Taylor's mother regarding her.

"I'm sorry about all that. Harold is a very passionate young man, and the nature of Taylor's departure left him soured."

Taylor stared at the table, mute, his cake forgotten on the plate in his hands. He looked to be more in pain than angry, as though an old ache was coming back to trouble him. "Mom's on the council," he said quietly, "as is my father."

"Among others." His mother smiled. "By the way, dear, I don't recall Taylor finishing his introductions. My name is Nikki."

"Angelica is a doctor, too," Taylor said, looking up finally, and trying to smile.

Nikki immediately brightened. "Really? Do you have a specialty?"

"General practice," Angelica said, quietly. The mug of coffee in her hands felt warm. Reassuring. Now that Harold was gone she found herself relaxing marginally.

"She's been working for Meadowlark."

Angelica's head shot up. He sounded... proud? She hadn't realized he felt that way about her work. Their gazes met awkwardly but he still smiled at her, the same way he had before... this last month.

"Meadow—Oh, that's the organization that puts up clinics in jungles, yes? That took over Doctors International. So you've been practicing somewhere remote, I take it?"

"Yes," Angelica said, not really wanting to go into it now that's she'd effectively quit. She still had no idea what she was doing next. Though meeting Nikki gave her a certain measure of hope. Maybe if other shifters could hold down normal jobs, it wasn't such a crazy thought that she could get this under control and do the same. "Do I take that to mean you're..."

Nikki laughed and waved the question away. "I haven't practiced in years. I mostly help out locally when someone has a headache or indigestion."

"That's because most injuries can be resolved by shifting." Taylor was speaking to Angelica, but his gaze never left his mother's face.

Nikki couldn't hide the gasp. Her eyes widened and her head swiveled to her son. She blinked and turned back to Angelica. "I hadn't realized that your relationship was so... committed."

"Mom," Taylor said, glancing uneasily in the direction Harold had stormed out, as though worried he might be lurking on the other side of the door. "We have a problem."

"I would say so," Nikki's voice, while still gracious, was a few degrees cooler.

Tell me this isn't just me noticing this. That there isn't a bias toward those of us who are... I don't even know what to call it. What's the shifter term for muggles?

"Angelica is having problems with her shifting."

Nikki blinked, then turned to Angelica. "My dear," she said, her voice surprised, her look assessing, "you are quite the surprise." She sipped her coffee, stalling for time. She looked at Taylor, several questions building in her eyes. "There is a legend about some of us, a precious few who struck out on their own ages ago. If she's..."

"No mother," Taylor interrupted. "She's a lioness. Not tiger."

Nikki looked at Angelica as if seeking verification. Angelica nodded and carefully set down the coffee before she spilled it. Oh, yes, this was going to raise all kinds of questions. She wasn't sure she was ready for this.

"And..." Taylor continued, "the shifting capability was artificially created. It was done to her without her permission."

Yeah, that ought to do it.

Nikki stood slowly. "Your father will be home for dinner, but not before. Why don't you two come with me. It sounds like you have quite the tale to tell." She paused and lifted an eyebrow at her son. "Angelica, dear, I wonder... there is a woman of my acquaintance whose opinion I would very much like to have. I wonder, would you mind if I sent for her?"

"No." Angelica shrugged. With the... cat... out of the bag, there was little point in trying to hide what she was. Word would get around a community this tightly knit quickly, she suspected. She might as well face the inquisition now, as opposed to later. "That's what I'm here for."

"Taylor, I wonder if you would be kind enough to give Mrs. Petrov a ride? Bring her around to the barn when you arrive, please."

Taylor nodded, and just like that left. He didn't even say goodbye.

Sick to her stomach and glad she hadn't tried eating anything after all, Angelica watched him leave. She saw him get into his truck from her seat near the window and wondered what would happen if he didn't come back.

It was a stupid thought. But the feeling of abandonment persisted, especially as Harold came up and blocked the view.

Chapter 6

S omewhat mystified, Angelica followed Nikki out to the barn. Why they were headed there she didn't know, but since Taylor didn't seem worried leaving her with his mother, she guessed it was safe enough. Especially as overprotective as he'd been with her lately.

Another problem that needed fixing. *But not now.*

Angelica had never actually been on a farm before. She looked around with interest at the flowers planted in front of the house, and the neat gravel path they were following down to where a red barn nestled into a hill a short distance away. Up close the structure was massive, far bigger than she expected. But even that was neat with fresh paint, right down to the white trim around the windows and door.

"You have a nice place," Angelica said, in quiet wonder. After the constant noise and hum of the jungle, or the racket of the refugee camp, this world seemed absolutely unspoiled. Even the birdsong, the hum of insects, was a soothing sound that chased away the noisy bustle of D.C. and the frantic energy of the airport that still seemed to buzz in her head. "I'm actually kind of a city girl. I grew up in L.A. Not that far from Hollywood."

"Thank you. It's our refuge." Nikki sighed and looked around. Her face seemed sad and her gaze lingered on the buildings, and the horses that ran in the distance. It was a lovely bucolic scene, yet Nikki had the air of someone saying goodbye. "This land wasn't easy to get," she said after a moment. "But we built it up, piece by piece, and it's served us well for many years." Her tone was wistful, and there was a certain mistiness in her eyes. "It would be a shame to lose it."

"Do you think you'll have to?" Angelica asked as Nikki braced herself against the barn door.

"I hope not. That'll be up to the council to decide. I just hope we all have the wisdom to face the hard choices." Nikki pulled the door open just enough for them to slip through, and led the way into the darkness of the barn. Angelica hesitated and then followed her in.

It was dim inside. Nikki hit a switch and lights flickered on. On the right was an open area with a dirt floor. Equipment, most of it defying explanation to a city girl, was parked in neat rows. A green tractor was recognizable enough, the rest she supposed had to do with planting and harvesting. Although she'd been working in several rural areas, in both the impoverished regions of South America and Africa, most work was done by hand. What this barn held would be considered true wealth in such places.

Shaking her head, she glanced to the left and saw what looked like a series of horse stalls. But these had high partitions between them. Several doors were open, a few were closed. It was the closed doors that caught her eye. They weren't what she expected to see at all, but were more like the doors you'd see inside a house not on an animal pen. Being taken out here to this suddenly felt creepy... and wrong.

Is this the part where she kills me and buries me under a pile of manure?

Only there was no manure smell. In fact, the smell that was strongest was almost antiseptic, with the soft intermingling of machine oil and a hint of dirt. That part at least she understood. A tractor should smell like dirt. And even oil. The rest?

Mystified and somewhat at sea about what they were doing there she turned toward her host, a whole slew of questions poised on her lips.

"I have some old equipment in here," Nikki said by way of explanation, leading her to the series of closed doors. "Taylor is right; we're a hardy lot and not prone to many maladies that shifting can't cure. On the other hand, on those occasions where someone needs special care..."

She pulled open one of the stalls. The inside had been converted into a sort of exam room, right down to a tile floor completely at odds with the rest of the barn. It was also very clean, the source of the antiseptic smell. The room appeared fully stocked to Angelica's practiced eye. However, whereas a normal exam room might have the majority of its supplies dedicated to the attention of injuries, small wounds or minor burns, this had few of those. Here the medicines on the shelves seemed to be concentrated on sickness, and digestive issues.

There was even a large electric razor mounted on a wall. *For shaving the patient?* She looked around the room with new eyes, realizing that it was indeed a cross between her own clinic's exam room and a veterinarian's office.

Angelica blinked. "I... Why in a barn?"

"Because," Nikki said with more than a hint of pride, "it's hidden. Everything about us is hidden." She smiled and took out a thermometer. "Taylor said you're a doctor. Have you given yourself an exam since this... whatever it was... happened to you?"

"It was genetic tampering," Angelica said, sidestepping the question. "Dr. Jones used a CRISPER to cut..."

"A CRISPER?" Nikki jumped on that. "On you? On a human? That technology's not reliable; there are risks. Horrible, terrible risks." She shivered.

"I didn't exactly volunteer for it," Angelica muttered, not liking the way Nikki looked at her, as though she'd *wanted* this to happen. "Neither did the entire village of locals who weren't as lucky as I was. For some reason, my alteration took. Theirs... did not."

Nikki stepped back, her face going slightly pale, her lips compressed as she realized what this meant. "I suppose after all these years it shouldn't still surprise me that humans can still do this to each other, but it does." She looked around the room for a moment, her body tense, uneasy. "I don't have anything nearly that sophisticated," she said slowly. "I can't do much about DNA. But I do know about the cells affected and the nature of that effect. I know that very well indeed."

"You're the doctor for everyone who..."

"Something like that," Nikki said, and to her credit she tried to smile, though the effort never reached her eyes. "Off the record, I don't have a license. But when one of our own gets in a bad way, it's often too risky to go to a traditional medical professional. Too great a risk of ending up in the hands of someone like your friend in Africa."

There was no censure in her words now. Just a quiet sadness.

"I'm sorry that you're at risk," Angelica said softly.

"Why don't we save that for the council meeting after dinner tonight, all right?" Nikki said, shaking off her maudlin mood as she reached for a stethoscope. "You neatly sidestepped my question of self-exam, so please allow a rank amateur to check you out, *Doctor*." She smiled.

Angelica was impressed. For someone without a license to practice Nikki was thorough, professional, and practiced. She had an easy bedside manner and the initial gathering of data, heart rate, blood pressure, all went the way they should. Thankfully everything came up normal, though Angelica had no idea what that would mean to the sleeping lion.

Nikki took a vial of blood and put a drop on a glass plate, that she might observe it under the microscope the next stall over. "I wish I had a better one..." Nikki murmured as she led Angelica into the next workspace. This one was set up like a lab, with a long counter on one side of the room, a small fridge, and racks of test tubes and vials, clean and waiting to be used. A case with glass doors held neatly labeled vials and bottles of solutions, giving the small space a feeling of being quite the lab, one that was every bit as good if not better than the ones in her own clinics. Nikki apologized for the crudeness of the facility, obviously feeling that it still had some failings in the small size, and in the lack of facilities. She snapped the slide into place and looked through the eyepiece, stopping her chatter mid-sentence.

"Same regenerative tissue. Same increased activity." She lifted her head and looked at Angelica. "You said you were having issues?"

Angelica opened her mouth to answer when the door to the room banged open with enough force to make her jump. An old woman leaning heavily on the carved wooden cane carefully crafted to look like a very long and lean tiger, stood there, positively bristling with barely suppressed rage.

"I can't wait to hear why an outsider is in your clinic, Nikki."

THANK GOODNESS TAYLOR stood right behind her.

"Angelica," Nikki said, drawing the other woman into the room and presenting her formally to the young woman, "Katerina Petrov. Katerina, this is Taylor's fiancée, Angelica."

A look of surprise flickered across Katerina's face. Angelica wondered briefly just what Taylor had told her when he'd gone to pick her up. Apparently not much.

"As charming as she is, and congratulations on your engagement, dear, why are we meeting here and not in a parlor or Margery's coffee house like civilized people?" Her tone was brusque, her eyes still suspicious.

"According to Taylor," Nikki said with a rather significant look at Taylor, who was hovering in the doorway. "She's a shifter."

She doesn't believe me. Him. Us. Whatever. Angelica shot a glance at Taylor, who was looking anywhere but at her. He'd been awfully closed-mouthed since they'd gotten to Minnesota. Hiding something.

Mrs. Petrov blinked owlishly at her. "You? A shifter?" She spoke quickly in a language Angelica didn't understand. Something Slavic. Maybe Russian? Angelica wasn't sure.

"No," Nikki said when the tirade finally ceased. "She's not from there. Apparently, our Angelica was the victim of genetic tampering. She was experimented on against her will."

The look on Mrs. Petrov's face was one of horror and disbelief. She crossed herself, a reflex gesture that Angelica nearly copied from the old woman's reaction, a holdover from her Catholic upbringing.

"They experimented on us in..." Katerina breathlessly and caught herself. "She's..." she turned to Nikki. "...a tiger?"

"Lioness," Taylor said from behind the old woman. Mrs. Petrov jumped. She'd apparently forgotten he was there.

"Lion?" she asked him, clearly confused.

"While in Africa," Taylor explained to the both of them, "we discovered a village of shifters. They shift into lions. A doctor there ran experiments on them and used those results to alter her DNA."

Mrs. Petrov looked suddenly much older, more frail. "I...I am so sorry, my dear." Whatever censure had been in her tone had disappeared. "I had no idea there were lions out there like us."

"And there were reports of leopards in the Amazon," Angelica couldn't resist adding, though she was less sure about this particular story until Taylor shot her a look of surprise.

He didn't know I knew. It was another interesting fact worth tucking away.

"Really?" Mrs. Petrov looked at Nikki and the corners of her mouth began to curl upward. "And here we were so convinced we were alone in the universe." She shrugged. "Nikki, what did you need me for? I have the council meeting tonight, and I haven't eaten yet."

"You can eat with us." Nikki crossed her arm and stared the older woman down. "I need you here."

"What are you having?"

"Rabbit stew."

Mrs. Petrov blinked. "Fine, I'll stay." Her tone made it very clear that she was doing *them* a favor by doing so. "What do you need?"

"What kind of problem are you having, dear?" Nikki asked Angelica.

"She changes without warning," Taylor said and Angelica flinched. Somehow hearing it like that made it sound like a failing on her part. "Like a pubescent. But the exercises aren't working."

Angelica sighed. Definitely felt like she was failing. Those damn exercises that he'd been harping on for weeks hadn't done her a bit of good. He'd been alternating between frustration and blaming her for not doing them right.

Maybe I can just go away and come back when they're done? Of course, he was only trying to help, but it would have been better to be able to talk about this, the two of them, before he'd decided to air it all like so much dirty laundry.

"Taylor, dear, why don't you get your bags and put them in your old room? We'll be along."

Taylor looked from one woman to the next as if he were a child who been asked to leave the room so that the grown-ups could talk. She could see in his face the moment he realized he *had* been asked to leave the room.

Angelica wisely bit her tongue, to keep from commenting on the rest of that thought.

Without a word, Taylor disappeared back through the doorway and was gone, whether he was lurking somewhere in the barn or had actually gone to take the bags out of the car. At this point she was rather hoping for the former, as the latter would leave them trapped here for the night and Angelica still wasn't all that sure she wanted to stay. Or that anyone else wanted them to either.

Speaking of welcoming committees...

Mrs. Petrov slowly approached her. Her walk was smoother now, all pretense gone. It occurred to Angelica that the reason Nikki flowed while she walked was the same reason this old woman glided even when she needed the cane. It was the cat. They moved like the cats they were.

Mrs. Petrov took Angelica's face in her hand and stared into her eyes. She looked so deep Angelica wondered what she was looking for.

"Do me a favor, dear," Mrs. Petrov said, releasing her. "Walk over to the door."

Angelica rose, headed to the door, and returned. Mrs. Petrov asked her to open her mouth and took a deep breath.

Finally she turned to Nikki, a frown creasing her brow. "I can't find her."

"Are you sure she's in there?"

Mrs. Petrov pursed her lips and looked again at Angelica. Finally, she shook her head.

Nikki nodded, like she'd been expecting that.

"Who?" Angelica didn't like the way they seemed to be talking without saying anything at all. So much passed between them in just those expressions, in the way of old friends who had known each other forever. Normally she wouldn't have minded but right now she felt very left out, especially since it was she they were discussing.

"The exercises are created to teach you to master the inner ti-gress—lioness. To control it, to meld with it. But I can't find yours. It's like..." Mrs. Petrov floundered for a moment, searching for the words. "For you, shifting is just like...like trying to tell your heart to not beat. It's purely physical. Without a cat, hmmm. Well, it's not shifting, it's..."

"It's going to get worse," Nikki said, interrupting her suddenly. "If that's true, then it's going to go from difficult to manage to impossible. And you'll start shifting at random."

"And you can partly shift," Mrs. Petrov said and shook her head. "Tell me, when you've shifted... how much do you remember from be-ing the cat?"

"All of it," Angelica said, not sure why that was such a big deal, es-pecially now that Taylor was melding with his tiger more. He remembered more from shifting than he ever had. Was she so terribly different?

The two women looked at each other. "How do you handle the difference in the body? It's a different balance, a different movement, things that should be handled by the inner cat. How do you manage?"

"I analyze the body," Angelica said slowly, working out the answer as she spoke. "I use a trick I taught myself in med school. My brain is eidetic."

"A what, dear?" Mrs. Petrov asked.

"Like photographic," she explained. "I remember medical facts. They occur to me, like triggers when I diagnose something. I use that part of my brain to manipulate the body. It's... like driving a complex car."

"That's going to work for only a little while, dear," Mrs. Petrov said softly, with a glance at Nikki for confirmation.

"Eventually, your body," Nikki explained, "will learn that it can heal from shifting. Without a cat persona to work that complex car, your body will take over the change and it will determine the when and where."

"Like falling asleep while driving," Mrs. Petrov added. "If you're tired enough, your body will sleep no matter what you're doing."

"So, I could change..."

"Without warning," Nikki finished for her.

"And..." Mrs. Petrov said, her large eyes filled with worry and compassion, "you might not be able to change back."

"How...how..." Angelica swallowed, feeling more uneasy by the moment. "How do I get this cat to listen?"

The older two women looked at each other. "That's beyond us, dear," Nikki whispered. "I've never experienced this. I don't know."

Mrs. Petrov shook her head. "I am so sorry."

Chapter 7

"Dad, this is Angelica. Angelica, this is Dmitri Mann, my father." Taylor made the introductions awkwardly, still unused to the words. And not entirely sure how the news would be received. He took a breath and added, "Angelica is my fiancée."

As it turned out, he shouldn't have worried.

"About bloody time!" Dmitri boomed, a huge grin splitting his face. It was a look Taylor had grown up with. His father's good humor was always the one thing he could count on. Even back when things had gotten difficult, he'd been one to find the silver lining in whatever black cloud Taylor had brought home with him. It was with thankfulness that Taylor realized that this hadn't changed, and that his father would accept him back into his life despite the long time apart.

"This is a wonderful thing!" Dmitri engulfed Angelica in a hug that seemed to wrap around her twice. As affectionate and warm as his mother was, Taylor's father always gave the Santa Claus of hugs; always plenty for everyone, and always given in warmth and adoration. This illusion was aided by the fact that Taylor's father was a large man—in every way. Tall and broad-shouldered, he stood about an inch or so shorter than Taylor, but still topping six feet. He had huge hands, weathered and callused from his work on the farm. He rubbed those together in delight now as he met Angelica, his eyes bright and interested, and warm. Most of his face was lost in a heavy beard that had more grey in it now than Taylor remembered. But he still moved as one who was young. Strong. His father was older, but not old.

He spoke now against her hair, his expression delighted. "It's a great pleasure to meet you, my dear!"

And just like that she was accepted. One of the family.

Taylor had to look away, swallowing hard to hide the sudden lump in his throat. He'd expected everything to be so much more like... well, like how Harold had reacted.

Angelica, on the other hand, seemed absolutely overwhelmed. Accepting the hug, but reserved. Withdrawn. Her eyes still wary. Wounded, the way they'd been since Africa. Whatever had happened in the barn had left her... the word that occurred to him was 'shattered.' He wondered what his mother and Mrs. Petrov had told her. She seemed to warm under the attentions of his father, though, thawing in his arms. But then, no one was immune to the old man's charms. He was genuinely pleased to see people and that delight showed.

"Thanks," Angelica said, stepping back from the embrace, a soft smile starting to play on her lips.

Taylor hadn't seen her smile much lately, and to watch it come back now was heartening. Maybe, despite all the tension, some good would come of this trip after all. He certainly hoped so.

"Where's Harold?" his father asked as he led the way to the dining room. The table was already set, Taylor's mother and Mrs. Petrov seeming to have things well in hand.

Taylor winced. "He said he was going to have dinner at a friend's house tonight." He omitted the other things his brother had added. Those words were between the two of them and not to be repeated. If there was to be any closure between the two brothers, it would have to start with discretion. Thankfully his father didn't press, though his sharp look seemed to say that he knew there was more to the story than was being told.

They sat at the table, Mrs. Petrov motioning Taylor to what had always been Harold's seat, while Angelica took his own. Taylor couldn't help but smile at the aroma of the stew. This was home to him. His mother did a good rabbit stew; it was one of his childhood favorites. She'd probably made it today in anticipation of his arrival.

They had planned the council meeting for tomorrow, giving him a chance to rest. He'd insisted that it be today, not knowing how much lead time they would have. Hopefully, the council would have some ideas that could help Angelica with her exercises. He needed to find out why she wasn't getting any positive effect from them.

That brought his attention back to her. He looked at her, smiling at something his mother said, eating with quiet enjoyment. She'd been different since their return from Africa. The ready smile, the quick wit, all seemed strangely muted. He'd thought it was the adjustment to becoming a shifter. He'd expected that. It was a lot to take in a single swallow; he'd had his entire childhood to mentally prepare for the change that came at the end of puberty. He was 16 before he changed for the first time; Harold had been almost 19. They'd thought he'd be an Exception, the rare one that never shifts. Sometimes the ability skipped a family member, and sometimes it skipped an entire generation. Harold's sudden change had been greeted with no small celebration, and equal parts relief.

The conversation droned on around him as Taylor spooned more of the stew into his mouth; he thought about his little brother and the widening gap between them. Harold not changing until so long after puberty seemed somehow appropriate to Harold, though Taylor would never voice the thought out loud. Harold wasn't the sort to take chances. And he certainly never took risks. Harold was stolid, unchanging, unflinching, and thoroughly dull. He had his routines and his world, and anything that disrupted those was cast into the classification as being 'bad'.

Taylor had shaken up the status quo when he left. He'd shaken it *because* he had left. Harold had yet to forgive him for that. But that wasn't the only thing about which Harold held a grudge.

It suddenly occurred to him that the conversation had stopped and the others were staring at him. He raised his eyebrows in question.

"I asked you," his mother said with exaggerated patience, "about your relationship to your cat."

Taylor blinked. "My... what?"

His father sighed and set down his fork. "It looks like neither of my sons is dining with us today."

Taylor set his utensil down, too. The clatter against the plate sounded loud. "I'm sorry, all of you—I really am. I was thinking of Harold and the gap between us..." He faltered to a halt, realizing what he was doing. It was so easy to fall into old patterns, to want mom and dad to step in and fix things somehow.

"It's going to take time, dear," his mother said, and he loved her for it; for the way that she didn't step in and try to solve things for him.

"I know." Taylor wiped his mouth with his napkin. "I'm just afraid that time is something we might not have much of. Now, what was the discussion I missed?"

"I was telling them," Angelica stepped in quickly, her hand taking his under the table, "about Melinda Johns and the pheromone spray and gene splicing."

Things he should have been paying attention to. She squeezed his hand under the table, letting him know it was okay, but it wasn't really. He shouldn't have been off woolgathering. These weren't easy things for her to talk about.

"Yeah... the spray." Now that the topic was in front of him, he realized it wasn't easy for him to talk about either. He cleared his throat. "Fortunately that stuff was destroyed, and her formula with it." He hesitated, and then voiced the thing he'd been thinking for a while now but hadn't dared to say out loud. "At least, supposedly it has."

"Supposedly?" his father echoed, frowning.

"Well," Taylor waved the word away, "I'm fairly positive that whoever talked about this to the military didn't have the data—at least, so far as I know they didn't. I think they'd be going about things differently if they did."

"Save that for the meeting, son," his father murmured, glancing uneasily around the table. "What we were talking about is teaching your lovely bride-to-be how we communicate with the cat. I was saying it can frustrating because it's always like some vague memory, and getting your cat to do what you want is..."

"I talk to mine," Taylor said, taking another spoonful of stew.

"What?" His father's head shot up and he almost dropped the roll he was buttering. "What do you mean?"

Taylor glanced uneasily around the table. Every last person was staring at him. "There's a voice in my head, most of the time, though lately he's not been around much. He doesn't like this body. Balancing on two legs is too tricky. Can I have some more?" He held out his bowl for his mother to fill from the pot resting on the table in front of her. She seemed not to see it. In fact, she was staring at him like he'd grown another head. One with fur. He lowered the bowl uncertainly. Dammit, why did he feel like a teenage kid again and not a grown man?

Yeah, that went well. Way to drop the bombshell. Remember how it hit you when it happened for the first time?

"You mean to say," Mrs. Petrov said slowly, "that you are in constant contact with your beast?"

Beast?

"With the cat, yes. But he doesn't like the word beast." Taylor rose and dished out more of the stew for himself.

"But—" Mrs. Petrov looked at him like he'd just offered to prove the ground and sky were the same thing. Whatever she was going to say, however, was cut off by the doorbell.

"Oh, good heavens," Nikki snapped, coming out of her trance. "Of course. Leave it to a bunch of Minnesota farmers to be early."

THEY ALL ROSE TOGETHER and Nikki fussed about the table, insisting that the food and plates be left alone, claiming she would take care of things after the meeting concluded.

The group followed Taylor's dad into the living room, Taylor carrying his bowl and still spooning the stew into his mouth. No way was he going to let that go to waste. He hung back as his father opened the door to three men and another woman, who came in all smiles and chatter. The woman had brought a homemade selection of pastries, and Nikki took it and went to put on some coffee.

This is not a particularly powerful group. It looks like a church social.

What would you know of church socials? Besides, when they get going...

I think I'm going to take a nap.

That's not a bad idea, actually. Taylor smiled, indulgent, as he wished the cat a good night. He looked up and found Mrs. Petrov staring at him.

"Ladies and gentlemen of the council, please let me reintroduce to you my son, Taylor. You all remember him." Taylor nodded to them all, remembering every one of them well. He'd grown up with them; one was the father of someone he'd gone to school with. The others were neighbors. Friends. He wondered how they felt about his intrusion now, but he couldn't read their expressions. His father took it upon himself to introduce Angelica, and Taylor realized belatedly that this should have been his job. Once again, he'd been distracted.

Not a good trait in an agent. *It's not just the tiger that's sleeping.*

"This lovely woman is Dr. Angelica Truman. She's our future daughter-in-law." Dmitri said the last part with a great flourish, and Taylor smiled at the effect it had. Their community wasn't all that large, and weddings were things to be celebrated. He became the victim of back-pounding and glad-handing as the news sank in.

Dmitri gestured for everyone to gather in the living room. He waited until everyone was seated to begin. The pastries were passed, coffee served by Nikki who stayed, balanced on the armrest of her husband's chair. "You all know why we asked you here tonight. If what Taylor says is true, then we have a grave concern."

"Of course, it's true," Harold spat from the door. "He brought them. He betrayed us. He showed them what we could do and then he led them straight to us!"

"Harold!" his father snapped. "You're not welcome in a council meeting. You know this!"

"HE IS!" Harold threw a finger at his brother. "AND SO IS SHE!"

The look he gave Angelica was pure poison. Taylor put his arm around her, letting her know that she was safe with them, that his brother had no power to hurt her.

He'd kill him himself if he had to.

Dmitri's eyes flashed fire. Apparently, Taylor wasn't the only one mad at the intrusion. "They are here on invitation to tell what they know. You are not, because you don't know anything anyone else needs to know. Now get out!"

"TRAITOR!" Harold snapped at his brother and, turning, stormed up the stairs. A moment later he could be heard clomping overhead as he went to his room.

"I'm sorry for the outburst. Harold's been having a rough time lately," Nikki said, eyes sad and disappointed. The group nodded without comment, though their expressions had shifted to something more thoughtful.

He's planted seeds of doubt.

"The floor is open to discussion and questions," Dmitri said with a pained sigh.

The female member of the council turned to Mrs. Petrov. "Is this the way it was? Did it happen just like this?"

Mrs. Petrov looked at Angelica for a long moment and nodded once, as if she had decided something. She settled more deeply in her chair, drawing her shawl up around her, as if to close out a chill that had nothing to do with the temperature of the room. "It was a very long time ago," she said with a sad smile. "The beginning of World War I to be precise. Over one hundred years ago. I was still a young woman, but I remember it too well. They came for us then, too. One of our number, Alentri, he was taken for the war, to be a soldier. They simply came to the village and took him, calling him our 'tribute to the war effort.'"

She shook her head. "As luck would have it, poor Alentri was shot. It hit him in the lung and he began to bleed, badly. He was far away from the hospitals they set up on the line, and there was no way to get him to safety. He was going to lie there and bleed out, like the others around him. He lay there in the dirt, listening to the screams of the dying, and knew that death was coming for him." She paused, her voice wavering a little. "He also knew that, if he shifted, he would live."

The group seated around the room exchanged glances. Taylor stared at his hands, holding a china plate with an untouched Danish on it that his mother had pressed into his hands. He'd been there, in the position of the young man, Alentri. He'd been shot, dying, and had known very intimately where survival lay. But to do so in front of those within his unit...

He licked his lips, feeling suddenly devoid of moisture. No. He couldn't judge this man for his decisions. Had he not also been making poor choices in the name of survival, in the name of Angelica's survival? It was truly impossible to know what you would do unless you were there. It had to have been horrific.

Mrs. Petrov bowed her head. Her face seemed to have aged in the telling of this story, the lines around her eyes, around her mouth, more deeply etched, wearing her age in a way she hadn't when she'd come into the room. "It's not that he didn't try. He suffered, writhing in pain and anguish until he thought he was alone. The battle had shifted, and he was behind enemy lines. They were using mustard gas. So he changed. The bullet was expended, the tear in his lung healed, the wound sealed."

Taylor winced. What an incredibly difficult decision that must have been. A shifter who tried to transform with something like a bullet within his body took his life into his hands. The bullet could lodge elsewhere. The heart, for example. The brain. What might have been a survivable injury could turn deadly if the bullet shifted to someplace more vulnerable.

"But Alentri was a lucky man. He was alive, but weak. And in shock. Only he wasn't alone like he'd thought. There were witnesses." She stopped and looked at each in turn, taking in the scowls, the expressions that held angry judgment on a man who had fought this battle over a hundred years ago. "You may say that you think he should have died rather than betray his people." Mrs. Petrov held out her hands, palms up, in supplication. "Maybe. But I beg you to understand. You haven't had to make that choice." She looked over at Taylor, her expression shifting, becoming more calculating, as though she saw things no one else did. Perhaps she did. "Most of us haven't," she amended. "Whatever the case, someone saw. Someone from the war department. Someone who thought that a man who can be a tiger should fight as a tiger all the time. As if fur and teeth and claws were a protection against bullets and bombs. But some people have to be proven wrong at the expense of others."

"What happened?" It was Angelica who asked, the others in the room too caught up in the story to ask.

"They came for us all then. They came in tanks and wagons and trains, and even horseless carriages." She smiled, a genuine smile this time. "But we fled. We all changed and slipped through the countryside in the middle of the night like cats dancing on shadows, and we fled the country. When we regathered, we ran again as humans. We came here. This was still so much a wilderness then, with only loggers this far north. Loggers and those who had been native to this place, who saw us and respected us for what we were, and bade us live in peace."

Mrs. Petrov dabbed at her eyes with a hanky pulled from her sleeve. "Alentri... he bought us the time we needed. In the end he died anyway. He gave his life to bring us that extra time, leading our pursuers off on wild goose chases, and when they caught him he gave them only misinformation, that his mistake could not be compounded further. For his reward, they dissected him instead of us."

She sighed sadly, and turned to Angelica. "My late husband was a hero. I want you to understand that. He gave his life for us." She smiled again, but this time her eyes were wistful. "He gave his life for me." She reached out and grabbed Angelica's hand. "I know you understand that."

Angelica patted her hand. "I do. But I'm confused. Don't you mean World War II? Even that would put you—"

Mrs. Petrov laughed and those around the room smiled also, for they understood the joke. Taylor winced, for he hadn't thought to tell her. "I'm one-hundred-and-sixty-two years old, dear."

Chapter 8

"Your mother doesn't agree."

"My mother has never seen an artific—a man-made shifter before. She doesn't have all the answers." He tried to keep his voice calm. Talking to Angelica didn't always make that easy. She knew how to make him frustrated. Him, and his cat, too.

"Neither do you!" Angelica sat on the edge of the bed and ran her fingers through her hair until it stuck out in all directions. "Taylor... we... I can't keep doing the exercises; they were made for someone who isn't *artificial*. They're not helping me." She threw a fair amount of vitriol into that word. Obviously, she'd caught his earlier half-usage. "Your mother and Mrs. Petrov said they were designed to communicate with the internal cat, and mine isn't realized yet."

Taylor took off his shirt and kicked off his shoes. "Honey," he said as he tugged on his belt, "you're not going to have one. Internal beasts only happen with the natural-born, not the way you got it."

"How do you know that?" She stood and began undressing. There was nothing seductive in her movements. This was the practical act of getting ready for bed.

He watched her and wondered if they were abandoning any sort of lovemaking for the night. The thought made him sad.

"You're the only one who thinks so. What if I do need to wake it, or activate it?"

"It's not possible," Taylor insisted gently. "I'm sorry, but what was done to you was done to your body. It was an alteration of the way your genes behave. There's no inner cat, because you weren't born to it."

"Then..." She threw up her arms in disgust. "Then there's no hope for me. I'm screwed." She plopped again, her jeans unbuttoned and gaping open. Her shirt lay on the chair. Maybe he wasn't supposed to notice when things between them were so tense, but he was struck by how intensely beautiful she was, how beautiful she always was.

He walked around to her side and perched next to her, reaching out to hold her hand. "We will find a way to control this," he whispered. "I swear it."

She groaned and leaned against him.

It was nice to feel her against him again, her soft hair tickling his shoulder. He kissed the top of her head.

The intimacy might have ended there. He certainly never expected more, nor would he have asked it, given how upsetting the day had been. But she turned to him and put her hand on his cheek, looking into his eyes for a brief moment before looking away. She seemed shy, uncertain. Maybe it was being in the house of his parents. Maybe it was because the tension was so thick between them. He caught her chin and brought her eyes back to his so he could try to decide which it was. She met his gaze unflinchingly, maybe a little sad. Very much frustrated. He leaned in, closing his mouth over hers, cautiously, letting her decide how much of him she wanted tonight. But her hand came up and cupped the back of his head, drawing him in closer, her mouth opening under his. Tongues met. Explored. Danced. He felt the familiar surge of passion that he only ever felt with her and drew her in closer, thanking God with every breath that, in all of this, he hadn't lost her after all.

She arched her back, her bare skin meeting his as she turned to face him more fully. He cupped a breast with the free hand and let his thumb roll over her nipple. She leaned into his touch and his hand fell, slowly, caressing her belly and dropping lower, into the opening of her jeans.

She broke off then, gasping with pleasure and arousal as he stroked her mound through the thin fabric of her underwear. For a moment she savored the sensation, head back with her eyes closed, lips parted. She gasped, held her breath a moment as he pressed just... there. She reached over and took hold of his manhood, stroking it slowly, showing him that turnabout was fair play. He groaned, the sound torn from his throat as she squeezed just so, right... there. Her hands were skilled, her fingers sure.

They half fell, half lay back on the bed, impatient as they moved up to nestle against the pillows. They needed each other too much to want to take time for even things such as that. Two battered and bruised lovers seeking to heal each other, wanting to be healed in ways that shifting couldn't do. He traced his fingers up toward her hair and then ran his hand from her neck, over her breasts and down the flat of her stomach, exploring her, memorizing her as though he hadn't already memorized her before. Maybe he hadn't. Every time with her was new, and lately even the lines of her body were changing. She'd lost some weight since she first became the lion.

He didn't need that thought right now. It was a distraction, an intrusion from the outside world they were trying so hard to escape. No, his attention needed to be here and now, in what they were doing in this moment.

So he concentrated on the one thing he truly wanted to. He let his lips follow where his hand had been. He touched and savored her every reaction. To his delight, she countered, finding ways to be closer, to make his own nerve endings sing with the electricity that always was when they came together.

It was sexual, but he realized that what they did was more than sex. He put into every touch that desperation to reconnect, to find that woman he'd lost under fire and under strain. He rose and pulled off her pants, sliding them down over her long legs and then stood between them. She lay beneath him, welcoming his body, welcoming him with the smile that he only saw in moments like this, when the passion darkened her eyes and gave her that sultry look that set fire to his soul.

He bent, kissing her, working his lips down the line of her jaw and over her throat. And in the end, he made love to her, slowly, gently, as though the pain and the aches were too fresh, too new to press.

When he entered her, it was slow and with patience. Her eyes followed his, half-lidded and bright. As he moved inside of her they closed, and she relaxed, letting herself go in the rhythm of the moment. He almost cautioned her about not changing, but when he looked at the beauty that was laid before him he held the words back. They had no place here, not where he reveled in the gloriousness of the woman who loved him, who was committed to him to the point where she wanted to spend the rest of her life with him. In a startling moment of clarity he realized that it was himself he sought in her flesh. And in understanding that, he understood what he had become.

Here he was, the man who had taken on an entire drug cartel in South America without flinching. He was the man who'd helped break up a slave ring in Africa. But somehow, he'd lost his hero status. He wasn't the man anymore who had won the girl. He wasn't the dashing hero who swept her off her feet.

He'd become a nagging mother.

Frantic now to prove he wasn't, that he could still be her hero, he increased his tempo. She wrapped her legs around him and pulled herself up against him. He reached out and lay his hand on her chest, above the breasts, and as he moved faster in her his hand reached up to cup her cheek, to hold the back of her head.

When he came, it was hard and deep. She followed quickly on the heels of his release and opened her eyes as her orgasm rolled over her, looking into his eyes with a wounded pride, an injured love. He felt her spasm around him, pulling him, milking him.

His heart cracked at the sight of her. Beautiful, naked, aroused, sated, and yet...

She looks lonely.

Taylor was startled. The cat usually didn't comment on people's facial expressions; they were too confusing for him.

You were there for the whole thing?

She's my mate, too.

It was a startling thought. Trying not to show the strangeness of his own emotions, or how unsettled he felt, he lay down beside her and took her in his arms, pulling her close. He stroked her hair and kissed her cheek and swore that he would never forget her and everything she meant to him, ever again.

This is what matters. Everything else can be worked with, adjusted. But this girl, this perfect girl in my arms, is naked, vulnerable, and trusting me to be there with her. For her. That's all that matters.

Somewhere, deep in his mind, a bass growl replied.

It was the middle of the night when the phone rang. He raised his head and listened as his father's voice echoed from the kitchen. Dmitri could never speak quietly to save his life.

"Hello?"

"WHAT? HELLO?"

Taylor slipped free of Angelica and threw on his pants. He met his father staggering through the hall. "What was that all about?"

"I don't know." His father shrugged and yawned. "Crank call I guess."

"What did they say?"

"They said... uh..." His father frowned as he tried to remember. "Something weird. You left your GI Joe on the front porch."

And just like that, the warmth of making love to the woman who meant everything in the world to him left. He stood for a moment, his body carved from ice as he struggled to say the words that would change everything. Not just for him, or even for his family, but for an entire community of people who had trusted him to keep them safe.

"Shit. They're here," Taylor said, his voice little more than a harsh whisper. "They've come."

Chapter 9

"**G**rab your bag!" Taylor burst into the bedroom and flicked on the lights. He grabbed her jeans from the end of the bed and tossed them at her. "Get dressed. Now!"

Angelica sat up, blinking sleepily. Her body ached, and she still felt the warm glow from the aftermath of their lovemaking. Her jeans dropped in her lap and she stared at them in confusion a moment, trying to remember where she was.

Then she knew.

He was throwing on his shirt as fast as he was able and had already slammed his feet into his shoes before she'd even gotten untangled from the blankets. Angelica jumped up and dressed as quickly as she could, pulling things randomly from her suitcase: fresh underwear, a t-shirt that didn't have the stench of travel in it. "What's going on?" She looked from him to the room, her gaze flicking from object to object, half expecting to see smoke or some other dire situation, though she knew deep down that the danger wasn't something so easily tangible. Her hands shook as she tied the laces on her sneakers.

They've found us. Somehow, they've found us.

His words confirmed her fears. "I had a signal worked out with Randall," Taylor said, grabbing his bag and dropping it on the bed. "The army's here; they're camped out at the road by the entrance."

"Camped out?" She echoed the words a bit stupidly, her sleep-filled mind still trying to catch up.

"They'll move in at dawn," Taylor explained. "With a tight perimeter around the property to ensure that no one slips away in the middle of the night."

Not quite the way things like this happen on TV. She shuddered. *Maybe I should be thankful for that. In every movie I've ever seen they come in, black ops, guns blazing, taking everyone out in the middle of the night.*

"What about all the people?" She grabbed her bag and slung it over her shoulder. "The houses... the livestock?"

"We're taking the dog," Dmitri said from the door. His shirt was unbuttoned, and he was wearing his boots untied. "The rest is under a protectorship. I already called the lawyer's office; they will deal with the assets as quick as legally possible."

They shouldn't have to do this. They shouldn't have to leave their homes, and everything they know. I'm the cause of all of this.

"Where will you go?" Angelica asked him, swallowing hard, trying to stamp down the guilt because it wasn't useful, and honestly wasn't all hers to carry much as her heart was trying to convince her it was.

"There's a place in Canada we have saved for just such an emergency. We'll be okay."

"If Taylor goes the hell away and stays away!" Harold called from the hallway. A door slammed. Thuds and bangs told her someone was packing hastily. Angrily flinging things in their haste to find what they needed.

Taylor's eyes flicked toward the direction of Harold's door. Angelica caught a hint of regret in their depths. "I sent a package to myself," he said, returning his attention to his father. "Did it arrive?"

Dmitri nodded. "I put it in the den. I haven't touched it."

Taylor nodded and slipped past his father, heading to the den. Angelica followed in his wake, not sure what else she should be doing right now. His mother was already there, hastily dressed, but she carried a large backpack with her. She pulled Taylor aside as he bent to retrieve the box from the desk.

"Taylor," she said under her breath, "Mrs. Petrov and I were talking. You need to take her to the elders." She nodded once in Angelica's direction.

"No, Mom." Taylor shook his head, adamant in his protest. "That's not necessary. She'll get the hang of it in time..."

"No, she won't," his mother snapped, and glared at him. "Do not ignore this, Taylor. This can become serious, and fast."

Angelica watched as Taylor opened the box and pulled out a pair of pistols and a carefully wrapped box of ammo. "I *am* serious," he assured her, "but we have maybe an hour before sunrise. They're going to come in force. You're going to need every pair of hands you can get."

"And we lose *everything*," Harold hissed from the doorway, "because you led them right to us."

"HAROLD!" Nikki snapped, without turning around. "Be quiet!"

"No!" Harold strode into the room, and for the first time Angelica noticed the shotgun again in his hand.

She flinched and stepped backwards, toward the wall, willing herself to not change, though right now she felt far too vulnerable as a human.

He's a tiger. And he's used to being a tiger. Do you really want to see which cat would be the stronger one in a fight?

She bit her lip, tried to keep from whimpering. Hating that she almost did. She used to be stronger. She used to be more sure of herself. Africa had stripped away all the best parts of herself and left only this... shell in place.

"He made the mess—we need to clean it up for him... AGAIN!" Harold paced, frenetic in his energy, eyes wild. Unstable in his fury. Unpredictable.

"What are you going to do, take on the entire United States Army with a shotgun?" Taylor hissed, getting in front of his brother, putting himself between him and her, Angelica realized.

"At least I'm defending my people, not betraying them!" Harold shot back.

Taylor shoved one of the guns into his belt and held the other out to Angelica. She recoiled, as if he'd just given her a snake. After her experience in Africa, she wasn't so sure she wouldn't prefer the snake. The gun felt evil, wrong in her hand. She pressed it back, not wanting it.

It made the difference between life and death there. His life, his death. It might again. "I... can't." Angelica looked up at him, her eyes pleading.

Taylor glanced at his father. Uncertain. "Here," he finally said, half turning to hold it out to him instead. His father took the firearm from him with a crisp nod.

"Don't you turn your back on me!" Harold snapped suddenly, grabbing his brother's arm and yanking him back around. Taylor swung at his brother and connected with his lower jaw. The sound could only be described as hitting a tree with baseball bat. Angelica flinched as Harold staggered backward. He caught himself on the edge of the couch and glared at Taylor, hatred in every line of his body. Raising the shotgun like a club, he'd taken two steps in Taylor's direction when Dmitri fired the pistol. Once. Angelica dropped to the floor, her hands over her ears. It took her a moment to realize he'd put a hole in the ceiling.

"Now they know that we're awake and armed," Dmitri said to Harold. "... and *that* is because of you. You're playing the fool, son."

Harold shot daggers at his father and stalked out of the room, his shoulder coming into contact with Taylor's as he passed, knocking him sideways.

Taylor clenched his fists but didn't respond.

Angelica stood uneasily, her heart pounding in her chest.

"Taylor," his mother said through clenched teeth, "you will listen to this. If you have never listened to anything I have ever said before, you will listen to me now. Take her to the elders."

"Mother, we don't have..." Taylor started to turn away, and jumped in surprise when she slapped him hard.

"LISTEN TO ME!" Angelica heard the snarl. Nikki was the tigress protecting her cub, the predator reborn. "Take her there, while you still can."

Angelica's eyes went wide. They were talking about her like she wasn't even there. And yet, she found herself siding with Taylor, wanting to go to his side, as though there were something he needed to be protected from.

Well, he *is* wearing a handprint across his face...

Taylor was mad as hell, eyes blazing. "What do you mean, 'while I still can'?"

Nikki looked at Angelica. "I mean, if her lioness doesn't awaken, her body—her *human* body will take over the transformation and you will lose her completely. She'll change, but Angelica won't come back."

"She doesn't have an inner lioness," Taylor argued. "She wasn't born to this, she was forced. Created. Someone did this to her."

"And that," Dmitri said, coming to stand with his wife, putting an arm around her protectively, "is why you have to. The elders are the best hope we have of reaching her."

Taylor stared at the both of them. The red handprint on his face stood out in stark contrast against skin that had gone deathly pale.

"Son," Dmitri said softly. Kindly. "Don't make me think I have two stupid children. Besides," he smiled at Angelica, who was trembling against the wall, "I kind of like the idea of having a daughter. And a lioness at that?" He chuckled. "Remarkable."

She smiled weakly. Yeah. Remarkable. *Wait. What does she mean I won't come back?*

The phone rang, Dmitri left to answer it.

Taylor looked at his mother. The anger had gone out of him. He slumped. Defeated. "All right. We'll see the elders."

Nikki reached up and lay her hand on his cheek, her fingers laying perfectly in the red marks her slap had raised on his skin. "Thank you, Taylor. Go as quickly as you can."

Taylor nodded. "We'll leave as soon as I see you safe in Canada," he promised.

"No need," his father said, coming back into the room. He thumbed in the direction of the hallway. "When you called yesterday and gave us warning, I spoke with the lawyer. That was them. They have a... writ? Injunction? I don't know, some damn thing that they're playing. They even woke a judge to back it up. It should buy us some time. I also installed some webcams around the town and at the entrance of the house. They're livestreaming on YouTube right now."

The whole scene was taking on a surreal quality. *YouTube?*

Taylor's grin nearly split his face in two. "That's brilliant!"

Dmitri shrugged. "I've been a pain in the ass for many years, son."

"Isn't that the truth," his mother said with a warm smile.

He laughed and bent to kiss her. "We're still running. It doesn't mean we don't have packing to do, it just gives us more time to do it," Dmitri said, but his expression was one of relief. "But while this will buy us time, you need to leave. Now. Somehow, I feel that all the legal documents in the world aren't going to keep you safe. And it certainly won't get you halfway around the world. You're going to need to get out of here, sooner rather than later." He shook his head and held out a hand to Angelica, pulling her into his arms for a quick hug. "You're going to be okay. I can see you're scared, and I don't blame you. We've been talking around you, and no one ever asks what you want to do. Listen to me, girl—no matter what you say or even think, there's a lioness inside you that's desperate to get out. I believe that with all my heart. The elders, they'll be able to help. Just give them a chance. Please?"

He released her and she stepped back, closer to Taylor. Dmitri didn't seem to be waiting for a reply, which was probably a good thing. She had no idea what to say.

Dmitri was already speaking again. "You can't go out the same way you came in, but do you remember Augustine?"

Taylor nodded. "Yeah, he's got the place at the other end of the clearing."

Dmitri nodded. "He's got his barn open."

It was a strange statement, but Taylor seemed to know what he meant. He looked wistfully at his mother and wrapped her in his arms. He gave his father a hug, and they in turn hugged Angelica. His father kissed the top of her head.

"Let us know," his mother said, choking on unshed tears.

"You, too," Taylor whispered.

Angelica blinked back her own tears. She'd barely met these people, but she'd come to love them in a very short time. It could very well be the last time they ever saw either of them.

Taylor took up his bag and looked at her, holding out his hand for her to take. Angelica smiled at the gesture and let her fingers entwine with his. He was her rock. Her stability. No matter what, so long as they had each other they would be okay.

Remember this feeling. When things get bad, remember this.

He led her outside without a backward glance and headed to the pickup.

Harold was standing in front of the truck, shotgun hanging over his arm.

The two brothers stared at each other for a long moment. Harold moved first, sidling away from the vehicle. Angelica's eyes never left the gun once as they closed the distance. She swallowed hard as they got close.

He nodded at them, face expressionless. "Good luck."

"You, too," Taylor said, returning his nod. He held out his hand. Harold looked at it for a long moment and shook his head.

"Not yet," he said finally. "Not yet. Just... let's get through this first."

Taylor's hand fell away. "It'll be there when you're ready," he said, and tossed his bag into the back of the truck.

Chapter 10

Taylor started the rental truck. It sounded impossibly loud, a roar that would carry forever in the quiet of the night. Angelica held her breath as he headed down the little road alongside the fields, his headlights off, startling the horses who thundered away in the darkness, each hoofbeat a thud she felt deep in her chest.

"How can you see where you're going?" Angelica braced herself in the truck. "There's not even a full moon out."

"Those exercises you hate so much," he said quietly, "teach you to activate part of the cat, like being able to shift one hand so you have claws. I'm using the eyes." He glanced at her and smiled. "Night vision."

"Handy." She stared out the window, wishing she could do the same but too scared to try. She couldn't face more failure this early in the day.

He nodded but said nothing.

She bit her lip, sensing she'd disappointed him somehow. After a minute she asked, "What did your father mean about the barn?"

"This community was constructed from the forest," Taylor said, raising a hand from the steering wheel to gesture at the wall of trees just beyond the perimeter of the field. "It was founded in a clearing, and a lot of logging was done to clear more space." He turned and headed west. The wheels bumped over another dirt track, rocking as they dove in and out of unseen ruts. It was definitely not a comfortable ride. "At some point they built up the remaining forest and put up defenses. That line of unbroken underbrush is deceiving—there's a fence under there, all the way around the town."

"Wow." Angelica thought about the little town of a few hundred people and how much space it took up. But in this case, it wasn't just the people; these were *farmers* with pasture and fields. The area he was talking about had to be enormous. "That's a lot of fence."

"And camouflage, and maintenance, and..." In the soft glow of the lights on the dash, she could see he was smiling at her. "There's even a moat."

"Seriously?" She blinked. "A moat?"

"It's what we call it. It's a ditch that we keep covered and... well, spiked."

"Spiked." She shook her head. Of course it was. Why wouldn't people put spikes in a moat? They must be expecting a battle. Maybe a war.

Wasn't that what she'd brought them? A war?

"It's not for people, but for vehicles. The only way to the town is that dirt track. Most people don't even see it. If you do get past the fence, your vehicle goes nose down into a deep, narrow ditch and the spikes make sure that your engine is toast."

"Clever." Horrific, but clever.

"They've learned from experience," Taylor said, and his voice sounded sad. And tired. "When we get out of here, I'll tell you about that."

She nodded, letting that topic drop. "So, what's with the barn?"

"Back in medieval times, churches and monasteries had all the wealth. They were often the target of thieves, like Vikings, Visigoths, highwaymen. So while the raiders were breaking down the gates..." He turned off the road and headed to someone's house. He sped up. Fast. "...the priests would run out the back through a secret exit. It was called a bolt-hole. Or a priest-hole."

The truck hit a pothole and, despite the seatbelt, Angelica hit her head on the ceiling. She yelped painfully. "TAYLOR!" she cried and brought her legs up against the dashboard, grabbing the handle over her head. He was driving at freeway speed and heading into an open barn. She closed her eyes just before impact with the far side of the barn, but fear had locked them open. As he drove in through the open door, there was a clunk. He had driven over a large flat metal sheet and the wall in front of them simply fell over.

The truck roared over what was once a wall, and she looked down to note that it had become a bridge spanning a narrow chasm. She saw metallic spikes shooting from the bottom of the channel. The foliage in front of them fell away a moment later, and after another head-crashing bounce they were back on the road that ran past the town.

"Where are..." She looked around, trying to get her bearings. The sky was lightening over the trees. Either that way was east, or there was a bigger military force assembling than she'd thought.

East. We'll call that east.

"We're on the other side of the town." He laughed, sounding relieved.

We're clear of the compound at any rate. But are we safe? That was when she heard the helicopter. *I take back my question.*

Taylor floored the truck, but he was limited to roads and the rental truck was white. Headlights or no, it was clearly visible. He took the vehicle as fast as he was able, the saving grace being a smooth, flat road. If there had been any turns at all, they would have flown off the edge of the street and into the ditch.

The helicopter backed off slightly, but Taylor didn't.

He slammed the brake with both feet and skidded to a halt at an intersection. The truck tried to slide sideways, but he fought the fishtail and ground it to a halt. He looked up out of the driver's side window.

"You're waiting for them to catch up?" Angelica gasped, her knuckles white where she was clinging to the seat.

"No," he said and pulled his head back in, turning the truck left and flying east, thankfully, definitely east, toward a sky that was becoming progressively lighter as the sun approached dawn. "I wasn't getting ahead. They were going to give up and go look for someone else to catch."

Angelica heard them then, growing close once more. This time, the thrumming of the helicopter's blades seemed to vibrate the truck itself. Taylor sped along, taking the truck to 80, 90, 95 miles per hour. The sun broke over the horizon and the helicopter broke off and headed back toward town.

Taylor slowed, gracefully this time, letting the truck wind down until it came to stop. Angelica could barely breathe.

Adrenaline: a hormone secreted by the adrenal glands, especially in conditions of stress, increasing rates of blood circulation, breathing, carbohydrate metabolism, and preparing muscles for exertion.

He got out and looked back, westward, as if he could see the town from here. "I hope they had enough of a window to get away," he said. He shook his head and sighed, then climbed back into the cab and took off again.

Her breathing was still ragged. She couldn't seem to find her way back to calm.

"Watch yourself," he warned her.

She blinked and automatically focused on being human, on dancing on two legs, on her back straight and tall. She felt the shift releasing her.

"You have to be more careful," he said, not looking at her. "There's no safe place now to hide. There's no place to change without being seen."

"I know that," Angelica muttered, trying to run the exercises in her mind. Not that they worked. But they did help her focus.

"Sorry. I know you know. I'm just worried." Taylor sighed. He tried to smile, to take her hand, but she shook him off, drawing her arms back tight around her middle. His reprimand had stung. Couldn't he see that she *was* trying?

"Who are the elders?" she asked, looking anywhere but at him.

"We're a long-lived people," he started, and stumbled to a halt, seeming to have difficulty finding the words.

She shot him a glance. "Immortal?"

"No, just longer than normal. It's something about the change and renewing cells constantly." He shrugged. "I suspect that'll change with you, too. That part is purely physical. So even your artif—your created physical change will most likely extend your life. The elders are like India's fakirs, or yogis. They've spent their lives researching the shift and how to exploit it, work with it. They're *really* old, more so than the rest of us will probably ever get."

"How old? Like they were there to see Moses being pulled from the reeds, or watch Troy fall?"

"Not that long." He shook his head, but he seemed uncertain. "All I know is that no one knows more about shifting than they do. Some people say that they can do things. Like, supernatural things."

Like shifting wasn't supernatural enough? "Like what?"

He blew air out of his nose, sounding frustrated. Not with her, but with the ability to not fully be able to answer the question to suit her. "I don't know; it's all nonsense, really. They're a group of old people with a great deal of knowledge. They seem mysterious so, naturally, there's going to be rumors about them." He rubbed his face. "I agree that they probably know more about shifting than anyone, but again," he waved one hand in the air as if trying to quantify the hesitation in his speech. "you're a... well, unique case."

She needed to ask, much as she didn't want to hear the answer. "What if your mother is right? What if I can't change back one day? What if my body decides that the lion is its natural function and I get stuck?"

"I don't know..." he said, and she could see he was just as frustrated as she was. "I think that might be..."

"No. Taylor, it's like..." Angelica thought of an example. "It's like being diabetic. Type two." *Diabetes mellitus.* "Your body doesn't make enough insulin, or you're resistant to it, but when you start injecting it your body decides it doesn't need to make any more at all, because it has an alternate source." *Other benefits of insulin include its effects on reducing triglycerides levels and increasing HDL. Not that that matters right now.* "If my body determines that shifting is good for my cells, it will revert to that rather than generating new ones. If I can't keep a disease that the feline body is immune to, then it will rely on that instead of creating antibodies."

He thought about that a moment and finally nodded. "I understand what you're saying. I don't have answers. I promised that I was taking you to see the elders. So maybe let's see what they have to say."

"What if—"

"I don't know!" He sucked in a sharp breath and let it out slowly. "Sorry. I'm just frustrated I can't control this."

Not as frustrated as I am. I'm the one who has to live with this. Not you. Angelica sighed and turned her head to look at the passing scenery. She spoke to the window. "I'm scared, Taylor."

She felt his hand take hers again. This time she didn't pull away. But she didn't respond either. Her thoughts were a million miles away.

"We need to get rid of the truck," he said after driving this way for several minutes. "It's too dangerous. By now they have a full description of it. There isn't a cop in the state who won't be on the lookout for it."

"It's a rental," she pointed out. "We can't just sink it in one of your ten thousand lakes."

He smiled. "I don't think it'll come to that. Randall will take care of the details. I'll get in touch with him. He'll just have to have someone fetch it from wherever we stash it. Not," he added, "from the bottom of a lake."

A sign ahead said PILLAGER–10 Miles. "I think there's a bus station there," Taylor said. "We'll drop the truck and get a bus to Duluth. From there we'll figure out a way to see the elders."

She turned to look at him, trying to ignore the fact that the name of the town left her with visions of Vikings doing Viking things. Didn't a lot of Scandinavians live in Minnesota? "Where are they?" she asked, more to distract herself than anything.

"Nepal."

Angelica blinked. "Nepal? Seriously?"

Taylor nodded.

Pillager loomed before them in the distance.

There really wasn't anything Angelica could add to that.

PILLAGER PROVED TO have all the appeal she had expected from the name. A market, two bars, a post office, and a volunteer fire station laid claim to the booming populace of 465 people, according to the sign. There was a bus stop on the main street, though the ticket had to be purchased at a mini-mart. She stared at a display of Paul Bunyan souvenirs, sandwiched between advertisements for LOTTO and a rack of Slim-Jims.

Taylor paid for two bus tickets with a company card, and the man behind the counter called him Mr. Summers after running the price of the fare. He never so much as batted an eye. Apparently, government conspiracies hadn't made it as far as this small-fry town. Angelica foraged, buying them juice and a couple of bananas that had seen better days, adding to the pile a few snacks that would keep them going until they got to Duluth. Rabbit stew with his parents seemed a long time ago.

He pulled their bags out of the truck and reached into his back pocket for his phone.

"We have four hours to kill," Taylor said, looking around the town with narrowed eyes. Looking for threats, she realized.

Not a thing moved on the streets, with the exception of a stray dog sniffing around the dumpster next to the mini-mart.

It certainly didn't have much to occupy their time. There was a little diner on the corner nearby, but even they hadn't opened yet. She dug in her bag and pulled out a banana and offered it to him. Taylor held up one finger and listened carefully to someone she suspected was a recording on the phone. He pushed a button and said the words 'Pillage, Rental, AT underway', and hung up, dropping the phone in the cab of the truck before locking the door. He dropped the key into his pocket and picked up both bags, waving off the fruit with a muttered, "Later."

"What was that all about?" she asked, tucking her purchases into her shoulder bag and following.

"Just telling Randall our status," he said, taking her hand and leading her across the street. "We'll wait for them to open," he said, nodding at the diner, "and get something to eat."

She eyed the restaurant dubiously. They hadn't eaten out since they'd gotten back to the States. "Aren't you afraid I might spontaneously change?" Her voice held more than a hint of sarcasm laced with anger that had been a long time brewing.

"Yes," he said bluntly, looking at the hours posted on the door. "But we do need to eat, and the truck was spotted. We have to ditch it."

Given it was the only vehicle parked on the street it already stuck out like a sore thumb, but she didn't say that. Where could he have stashed it? There wasn't another car in sight, with the exception of a delivery truck that had pulled up at the mini-mart and was unloading crates of milk and juice from the back.

"Four hours. That's a long time." Angelica leaned against the window of the restaurant, crossing her arms and watching as the stray dog went to lap water from a puddle down by the road. "Isn't it only a matter of time before they figure out where we went? It's not like we passed through a lot of towns on the road."

"Probably," Taylor said, "but we're safer in public, such as it is." From the scowl on his face, he didn't like it any better than she did. He stared at the deserted streets, vigilant. Alert. "At least it's better than if we were still on the road somewhere. Out there we're vulnerable. And the next sizable town is several miles from here."

The door opened behind him. An older man leaned out to look at them. He was grizzled, lean, and wearing a blue uniform shirt that said 'Carl' on the chest just above the pocket. "Can I help you folks?"

"We were just wanting to get a bite before the bus comes." Taylor smiled politely. "Just waiting until you opened."

The man looked over his shoulder at the clock over the counter. He looked back at them, forehead creased. "Huh. Long wait, I bet. Come on in, then." He retreated behind the door, holding it open that they could walk in. The inside of the café was neat and spotless, if well-worn. The tile floor had a path cut through the linoleum at the door, the result of years of mud and snow-encrusted boots and endless mopping.

Four booths comprised the dining area, though the counter would hold another six. There were only five stools, though, and one tall chair that might have once belonged to a different place, but had been pressed into service to replace the stool marked by four holes in the floor where it had once been installed.

The predominant color of the café was a light orange and brown with the occasional silver of duct tape highlighting old wounds in the upholstery. Taylor took a seat on one of the stools near the door.

"I was just setting up." the old man said. "Coffee isn't ready yet, but I don't expect that to take too long. I don't usually open for another half hour at least."

"Thank you for opening early." Angelica placed her bag on the floor and perched next to her fiancé. The old man waved in acknowledgement and reached up to slap the power button on the television. It flared to life, the screen turned black and slowly resolved into an image of a weather map and someone pointing to series of concentric circles, talking about the next six days being warmer and sunnier than the previous six days and ending up with a joke that went over Angelica's head.

By the time the coffee was done and the old man had placed a plate of eggs and bacon and slightly burned hash browns in front of each of them, the television featured a children's show host who alternated between condescending and cloying.

"What does AT mean?" she asked Taylor as she spread jam on her toast.

He looked up at the kitchen, but the owner of the café was busy with his preparations for whatever morning rush a town this size offered.

"You said it on the phone just before we got here," she prodded when he didn't answer.

"Oh. Alternate Transportation."

She poked some of eggs across the plate. Oddly enough, she wasn't as hungry as she'd thought. Somehow even asking had brought back the reminder that things weren't safe. That they were still very much in danger. She stared at congealing bacon grease. "Are...are they going to be okay?"

The door suddenly banged open, bells jangling wildly announcing the new arrival. "Hi, Dad!" A woman came smiling through the door and hesitated when she spotted them. "Well, hello! You're here awful early! Or I'm awful late!" She waved as she walked past.

"You? Late?" the old man called. "You're always exactly fifteen minutes late to everything, May. I just never figured out how you time it so precisely."

"Oh, hush!" May waved him off, but she was still laughing. She ducked behind the counter, dropping her purse somewhere out of sight, and grabbed an apron from somewhere, pulling it over her head and tying it securely behind her.

Angelica judged her to be in her early thirties. Her doctor's mind watched her with interest; she was very plump but she moved with the grace of a dancer. Her hair was jet black, but there were copious amounts of grey streaked through, creating swirls of highlights pulled away from her face and tied back into a bun. She had crinkles in the corner of her eyes suggesting she laughed often, but there was a deep sadness about her that Angelica couldn't identify.

There was something else, something that gnawed at her, but remained stubbornly just out of grasp.

"Here ya'll go!" she chirruped, leaning forward to refill their coffee. She disappeared to track down more cream for Taylor, returning a moment later, a testament to her efficiency. Satisfied that there was nothing more to be done for her customers, she grabbed a rag and a spray bottle and headed off to do battle against all dirt and disarray, whether real or imagined.

Taylor waited until she was gone to answer Angelica's earlier question.

"This isn't the first time for most of them," he said under his breath, with a wary glance toward the waitress.

May. Her name had been May.

Angelica glanced at him, startled. She'd been trying to worry at the puzzle of the waitress and had nearly forgotten her question. "What do you mean?"

"Let me amend that. It is for Harold and for me. But for my parents and most of the others, this is something they've done before."

Angelica nodded and returned to organizing her eggs. "I'm sorry, Taylor. I..."

"Dad! Come out here quick!" May called, and reached for the remote. The cloying children's host had been bumped for a news bulletin. The scrawl line said something about a small community having been quarantined by the army. It also gave the location of the community, a pocket of farms located in the Minnesota woods, fifty miles or so from Pillage.

"I'll be," May said shaking her head. "And they're not saying what they're quarantined for." She shook her head. "All I know is that if it's something like that plague, I want to know so I can get my precious babies *out* of here."

"Ain't no need for that," the old man said, returning to the kitchen, uninterested in something so far outside of his world. "They got it all under control."

"...attorneys for the co-op have vehemently denied any such measures, and are demanding that officials provide a clear explanation for the interference." The woman behind the desk froze, blinked, and waited. After an uncomfortable moment, another woman appeared on the screen. This one stood on a staircase outside of a large building in a city, presumably Minneapolis, and was surrounded by reporters.

"There is zero evidence of any sort of threat or menace either to health or otherwise from our clients. The military has simply moved in without provocation and attempted to overrun a peaceful farming community, and we demand to know the reason." She was then replaced by an artificially enhanced image of trucks and uniformed soldiers milling around the opening to the farmhouses and froze on a single image. "This is footage from a security camera outside the farming compound," the newswoman said. "This man is Major General Willette." The grainy image was replaced with a stern-looking man in uniform with enough medals to sink a small rowboat. "General Willette is a part of a research team from the Pentagon—"

May switched off the TV. "Ain't that just the thing?" she said, shaking her head, and went to refill their coffee to find that they hadn't had a chance to finish the last warm-up.

"Excuse me," Angelica said. "I don't mean to pry, I-I'm a doctor." She stopped herself and smiled at May. "May I ask, have you been having any upset stomach lately?"

"Wow." May blinked. "I don't know where you practice, but I think I want to come to you from now on! How did you know that?"

Angelica felt Taylor's hand on hers, squeezing. A warning?

"Just an educated guess. You probably should get that looked at. Have your doctor order an Alpha-Fetoprotein screen."

"Alfa which, now?"

"Just tell him you want an AFP." Angelica smiled. Taylor's hand was all but crushing hers.

"Can we get the check, please?" he asked, all smiles, sipping his coffee with exaggerated cheerfulness, but clearly mad as hell.

Chapter 11

"What the hell? I can *smell* cancer now?" Angelica hissed to Taylor's back as he crossed the street. He was still mad from the way he carried himself, rigid as a flagpole. Worried, too. That news report—everything was crashing down all around them, and she'd found a new skill.

"Among other things," Taylor said. "Yeah." He headed back to where they'd parked the truck and pulled out the key.

"I thought we were taking the bus." Angelica was confused. Suddenly, without any discussion at all, he was changing all the rules again. Since when were they running again?

"We were," he said unlocking the cab, "but that was before you started to change."

Angelica froze on the street. She checked her arms, her hands, what she see could of her legs and feet through the jeans and shoes she wore. She felt normal. She felt human. "I'm not..."

"You are," Taylor insisted. "Internally. Get in."

Mystified, Angelica looked at the truck and back at him. Taylor was acting like an angry parent and was casting her in the role of the belligerent and not too bright child. She suddenly felt tired. Tired of the fear and the stress and obligations of shifting. And tired of not being a partner so much as something that needed caregiving. Even his parents had done it, with that entire conversation this morning about taking her to the elders. Why was it no one ever just came out and asked *her* what she wanted to do? She wasn't even being allowed into the discussions at this point.

No way in hell was she going anywhere without some answers.

"Explain," she said stubbornly, crossing her arms.

"Your olfactory senses shifted," he said, glaring across the bed of the pickup at her. "Get in."

She stayed right where she was. "So, like a cancer-sniffing dog?"

"Not as good, but yes. Like that," Taylor said. "Get in."

"I am not changing." Angelica dropped her bag on the pavement beside her. "And I'm not a child. Don't treat me like one. I'm very sorry if..." she swallowed hard, "...if I've been the cause of your problems, or if I created problems for your family..." She glanced down and noticed she was shaking. She couldn't stop the tremors in her body. Damn it. This was all his fault. Why wasn't anyone listening to her anymore?

Taylor came around the truck and wrapped her in his arms and held her. How could she hate someone and love them in the same moment? But the truth was she needed a hug, and so she leaned into his chest and put a hand on his arms and bit down on the rest.

"Come on," Taylor said after a moment, stepping away to pick up her bag and heave it into the bed of the truck. "Let's go."

"No!" Angelica stepped away from him, staring at him through vision blurred by unshed tears. Here she'd thought that maybe she'd finally gotten through to him, to reach him, to be able to tell him all about the terror and self-blame she lived with every single day, but in the end she'd failed. In the end he wasn't listening to her after all.

She grabbed her bag and stalked off. The bag thumped hard against her thigh. "I'm done. I can't live like this anymore. I...I don't know, but I just..." She turned to him, her eyes searching for something, anything she could latch on to, something that she could use as a lifeline. Some way to save herself from becoming so lost that she forgot who she was inside.

But to just get back in the truck? No. How could she go back to a life of running and panic and waking up in the middle of the night, frightened and alone and deep in nightmares she couldn't tell anyone about? It was a hell. Taylor was her love, her soul-mate, but this had changed him, too. Somehow, she'd lost the conquering hero, the bold agent who had swooped in and swept her off her feet.

I haven't seen that man in forever

Or had he ever truly existed? Maybe it was just the way she'd wanted to see him.

"I miss you. The real you," she said quietly. But she couldn't think what else there was to say, and so she turned and walked toward the end of town.

"Wait!"

"For what?" She turned around, still standing in the middle of the street, her sneakers balancing on the yellow line that divided the road. "For my exercises? For being reminded that I can't handle what's been done to me? What do I wait for, Taylor? Until I turn and can't turn back again? What will you have me do?" She stepped up to him, trying so hard not to scream at him and lash out and say all kinds of things she would regret later. But at the same time she wondered if that was the key, the mysterious way to reach him that she hadn't been able to discover thus far in their relationship. Her voice softened. "I understand that you had all the training, and all the prep time to understand what you were before you even sprouted your first whisker. I understand that you've had years' more experience than I'll ever have. I get all that." She sighed and looked at the pavement as she struggled to collect her thoughts. "But I thought, I *thought* we were partners in this. When we—when *I* shot Dr. Johns, I did it to protect my love, my partner, my equal. When we ran through the jungle together, when we went through torture at her hands, when we searched for survivors and ran through the rainforest, we did it together."

She stared up at him, desperate to see something in his eyes that would have all the answers. "What changed?" She nearly wailed that question, all the grief and disbelief and concentrated fear that had plagued her dreams and every waking moment slipped through in that one question. "I lost myself, my definition of myself, everything I thought I could call myself. I have this *gift* that will curse me. And most of all, I lost you. Why?"

"You didn't lose me," Taylor insisted. His expression was one of confusion. The skin around his eyes sagged, giving his face a haggard, sad look.

Angelica sighed. "Why? Because you're here with me? You're not here. You're on the road, you're on the phone with Randall, you're two steps ahead of the bad guys, but *you're not here*! Taylor, I might become a lion and not come back. Can you grasp that? I might be stuck forever. And my best hope is in Nepal? People do not go to Nepal! You're born there, or you visit as a photographer for *National Geographic*, but otherwise *you do not go to Nepal*!"

"My ancestors..."

"You ancestors *left*. For a reason!" She bent forward, burying her hands in her hair, scrunching the strands in anger and frustration, trying not to scream. "Taylor. Please..." She raised her head to look at him, truly look at him. "Please, come back. Just a little. I'm scared."

For a moment she thought he wasn't going to come. She stood, her hand out uncertainly in his direction, waiting, her heart breaking with each second that it took him to move.

Subdued, shamefaced, Taylor nodded and reached for her. She grabbed his hand in hers. That became a lifeline, a bridge across the chasm that the stress had created between them. She held on tight.

"Let's go," Taylor said finally, drawing her back toward the truck. "We have a long drive..."

You have got to be fucking kidding me.

Angelica threw her head back and closed her eyes and counted to twenty. A benefit of higher education was the ability to do it in Latin.

"Angelica?"

"...decem, viginti." She opened her eyes and looked up at him. "Fine," she whispered, her shoulders slumping, defeated. "Fine, let's go..." She shook her head and reached for her bag.

That was when the siren sounded.

They looked back the way they'd come and saw a single police car, its lights flashing. It had given a single WHOOP of the siren and no more as it cruised up to them. "Get in the truck," Taylor told her, pressing her behind him.

I'm back being the Girl Scout in a forest fire! Damn him! All that and I was so sure he listened...

Angelica stomped to the truck and dumped her bag in the back. Taylor stood waiting for the cop to draw even, his stance easy, hands out, showing he was unarmed. To a casual observer he was calm. His body language screamed that he was harmless. Only she, who knew him so well, would recognize the tension in his shoulders. She stared a long moment, remembering the gun hidden in the small of his back, hating the sick feeling that started in the pit of her stomach and spread. Her heart pounded in her chest, her hands unsteady, and cold.

I can't do this.

They were far enough away that she couldn't make out everything they were saying. The cop leaned out the window of the car, less like Andy Griffith and more like... well, someone with harder edges. Any second now his attention would shift to her and what would he see?

Turning her back on the truck, Angelica started walking. There was no destination in mind, no hiding place where she could just disappear. If the entire U.S. military machine was swooping down in the form of one small-town police cruiser, then maybe this wasn't the threat she'd thought it was.

She needed air. She needed time alone. She hadn't been without Taylor at her side for over a month. *Funny, that used to sound like a sweet arrangement.*

Now it wasn't. She was suffocating.

There.

It was surprising that in a town of fewer than 500 people, surrounded by woods, there was still the need for a municipal park. It looked like something out of a 1950s postcard. An old-style gazebo was in the heart of the grassy space, surrounded by a handful of benches. She pictured a band playing there, off-key, on summer evenings while children played on the swings and other equipment just opposite a small building that housed restrooms. But it was still early, and there were no children playing, no happy crowds to get lost in. Just a young woman walking her dog.

Maybe that was what she needed all the same. Some time. A little peace and quiet. A moment without lions and tigers and leopards and drug tsars and generals and whatever else.

Angelica headed to a bench, not seeing the gopher hole until it was too late. Her foot dropped into the pit and twisted; she felt the sprain and dropped hard, down on one knee.

She felt the pain lace up her leg. Her foot felt as if it was dipped in acid.

"NO!" she screamed, but it was too late.

When confronted by illness or accident, the body will direct all available resources to heal or correct the problem. This astonishing ability to shunt calories or blood flow or anything needed to preserve the body is remarkable in that—oh, shit!

"GOOD MORNING." TAYLOR smiled his biggest smile and strode to the police car, keeping both hands in sight. The cops were the last thing he needed, and as of this moment he had no idea why he was being called onto the carpet. The only good news was that if this guy had any suspicion he had anything to do with that mess on the morning news, he wouldn't be confronting him alone.

Something else then. Play it cool, Taylor. Find out what he wants and then leave town all nice and quiet- like.

"'Morning." The man wore a uniform with the word SHERIFF emblazoned on one shoulder patch. He looked to be in his late fifties, and had a worn look about him. Yet he was cautious. A professional at odds with the small town. Taylor took him for someone who had, perhaps, taken this job as a way to escape a busier urban area. "Can I ask why you're in the middle of my street?"

"Just having a little lover's spat. And I'm apparently losing again." Taylor shrugged, only too aware that it wouldn't take much to get called on a domestic just because this Mayberry cop was feeling a little bored and needed something to do. "We just came out of the diner over there." He thrust out his thumb, pointing back at the restaurant where May and her father were undoubtedly watching the drama unfold on their little street, given the dearth of customers this early.

Keep it cool. Let him know that we have money, that we supported a local business. That this is nothing to get excited over.

The mate is walking away.

Of course she was. Why would she start listening now?

I have to deal with that later. Track her.

"I know that it may not seem like much," the sheriff was saying, "but this is a main road and I would appreciate it if you could take your arguments to the sidewalks."

"Yes, sir, of course." Taylor nodded, trying to keep his face neutral when inwardly he was ready to drop- kick something into the next county.

"Is that your truck?"

Taylor looked at the rental and internally sighed. So much for not drawing attention to the vehicle. All he needed was for this guy to run the plates. He certainly couldn't lie about it. The old man at the diner and the kid who'd had to read a manual to sell him a bus ticket had seen them pull up in it.

"Yes, sir," Taylor said, keeping his voice light. "It's a rental, at any rate."

The sheriff nodded, thinking this through. "Well, you don't seem to be indigent at any rate. Just keep to the sidewalks."

"Of course," Taylor said and waved his thanks, heading for the truck as though he hadn't a care in the world. He looked down at Angelica's bag in the bed of the truck and let out the breath he didn't realize he was holding. She wouldn't have gone far without her stuff.

Where is she?

She's close. I can run there quicker... oh, fine. Around that corner. She's changing.

Taylor's head came up sharp. *Changing?*

Taylor threw his bag and took off a dead run. He rounded the corner and spied a small park ahead, just past a bank that looked like it was built in the early 1920s, though it boasted two working ATMs built into the wall. The contrast to the building was jarring, distracting, and made him think of Las Vegas.

Of Angelica, there was no sign.

Cloth. There.

That startled him. The cat was getting more and more active when he was in human form. To point out things he'd missed was disconcerting. But handy. Taylor raced over to the area indicated. He found her shirt, shredded. Her jeans had survived the transformation somehow, but the button was still fastened, and her shoes were also in remarkably good shape.

She is learning to slip out of them. The cat's voice seemed proud.

Where is she?

He scanned the area. On one end was the bank he'd seen, on the other was a small building with the words COURTHOUSE carved on the lintel.

Someone screamed.

Taylor ran in that direction and nearly toppled a woman running the other way, carrying a small dog. She paid Taylor no heed. She likely wouldn't have noticed him at all if he hadn't been blocking her path.

She rushed past, screaming, the dog yipping a hundred miles an hour, excited and struggling to get free from her grasp.

Taylor headed the direction she'd come from.

STOP!

Taylor froze in his tracks. Again? What had he missed this time?

"Taylor?" Angelica's voice hissed from somewhere nearby. "Taylor?"

Several houses fronted the park, small places that dated back to WWII, the type of bungalows meant to be starter homes, wood-framed and likely picked out of a catalog. Just across the street, a wood-framed construction was almost hidden behind an elaborate arbor that led into a yard that was a gardener's dream... or nightmare depending on how you wanted to look at it. Shrubs of all kinds fronted the road; behind were vast beds of flowers, and more bushes lining the space just beneath the windows. Everything was growing in wild disarray: the bushes hadn't been trimmed in a long time, the flowers were a bright splash of gaudy color with no rhyme or reason to the design.

Anything could have hidden in that wild tangle. Including one very terrified cat.

Or a naked woman, as was now the case.

Sure enough, Angelica was crouching low in the bushes where they grew wildest, just below the windows. She pressed against the wall of the house itself, wild-eyed and angry. Probably more with herself than anything, though her moods lately had become unpredictable, and more often than not he'd been found in the wrong when, to his way of thinking, he'd done nothing at all.

Right now, though, was no time cast blame.

"Oh, shit, thanks!" Angelica cried when she spotted what was in his hands. "You brought my clothes! Thank you!"

He tossed the clothing over the top of the hedge, glancing uneasily back at the street. It was only a matter of time before the hysterical woman found the cop. They had to get out of there. Quickly.

"My shirt!" Angelica cried out suddenly. "I can't go around topless! I didn't even have time to put on a bra this morning!"

The fact that she'd been wearing one at all was still a point of contention between them. He'd been wanting her to go without since that day in D.C. when she'd nearly strangled after transforming unexpectedly while wearing one. She'd argued that she didn't like how her breasts had bounced when she didn't. He'd pointed out that he rather liked her bouncy boobs, and things had degenerated from here.

He opened his mouth to say something, thought better of it, and instead pulled his shirt over his head. "Here." He tossed it to her.

Unfortunately, they must have been talking too loudly, because the window behind them flew up and a very sleepy face appeared. The girl had to be 14, maybe 15. She saw Taylor under her window without his shirt and screamed. And continued to scream.

Angelica bolted through the bushes, making the screaming worse, and they both ran back toward the bank and headed for the truck. For once Angelica wasn't arguing with him about where they were going. There were some shouts behind them—apparently the girl's father was in hot pursuit.

Taylor had the truck fired up before Angelica could get into it, and they were halfway to the next town before he realized he was sitting on the phone he'd used to notify Randall where they were. Assured that the sheriff hadn't followed them yet, he pulled over long enough to pull a shirt from her bag and reclaim his. Standing on the road next to the driver's side door, he dug around in the seat until he found the phone. He'd felt it, but it had slipped down into the seat. Finally wrenching it free, the momentary elation he'd felt was immediately squelched.

The screen on the phone was now shattered, a hundred little lines going in every direction.

Of course. Why would anything go right?

Fighting the urge to say some very choice words, Taylor dug in his bag for a cigarette lighter.

"What are you doing?" Angelica asked, peering at him through the open window of the truck.

"I bought these under an assumed name." He held up the bus tickets. He dug through his bag and unzipped a pouch in the lining that was nearly impossible to detect upon casual inspection. He pulled out a small envelope—about the size of a credit card, only thicker. He took his wallet and removed the driver's license and two of the credit cards. He then replaced them with the contents of the envelope. "But if I try to use them again, they'll be able to track us."

With the lighter, he carefully set the tiny flame against the tips of the bus tickets and gently blew to start a fire. The tickets caught. He dropped them onto the pavement and added the old driver's license, as well as the two credit cards, to the tiny pyre. They melted, though not completely. At least it was enough to obscure the number and the name. When the fire died he stamped on the remains until it was no longer smoldering, and buried the mess in the ditch at the side of the road.

"I'm sorry," Angelica said miserably as he stomped back up to the truck.

He shot her a look. He really wasn't in the mood for apologies. "What happened back there?"

"I just needed some space!" She threw her hands up in frustration. "A little time without running, without fighting or having to constantly do exercises or... well... anything." She looked at the farmland and the neat rows of roses growing on the other side of the street. "Then I twisted my ankle."

He shot her a look. "That's it?"

She nodded. "Yeah, it was a bad sprain." She closed her eyes and carefully started reciting. "*Hyperextension of the muscle, partial or complete tearing of the ligament can include a tearing or 'popping' sound, swelling as injured blood vessels leak fluid into local tissue. The body re-*

leases endorphins and body will begin healing the... But it didn't, did it? Not in the traditional way."

"You changed over a twisted ankle?" Taylor repeated, half of what she'd just said washing over his head, a tidal wave of just so many words.

Balancing on two legs is asking for it.

"My body healed itself." Angelica was speaking like a doctor now, clinical. Sure of herself. "It figures that shifting is the fastest way to heal, and so it started the process when I wasn't even thinking about it. All I could think of was the pain. It was excruciating."

See?

And my body just changed. I didn't even realize it until I found my-self stalking a woman and her dog. Oh, shit. Taylor?"

"They're fine. She was pretty shaken up. The dog was about stran-gled in her arms, she was holding him so tightly. But that's a witness. Someone saw you change. By now she's not only told the authorities, but anyone else who will listen as well."

"I know." Angelica slumped miserably in her seat. "Why don't you?" she asked him. "Why don't you shift when you're hurt? You've told me about long recovery times in high school and on the farm. Why doesn't your body make that same decision? What is it about me that my body does?"

Because that isn't his body, it's mine.

"I don't know," Taylor said, climbing back into the truck.

Liar.

Taylor fired up the truck and headed back onto the road, the ashes of his former identity buried in a shallow roadside grave.

Chapter 12

Mr. and Mrs. Langtree boarded a Greyhound in Bemidji heading for Duluth. Bemidji was an unexpectedly largish place, at least in comparison to Pillage. At almost 15,000 people, downtown consisted of several streets and businesses, and this time the truck was parked behind a hardware store.

Angelica was surprised they'd gotten as far as they had so quickly. She'd been sure they would be plucked from the road and made to disappear before the truck could even come to a complete stop. When she voiced this to Taylor, he smiled. It was the first genuine smile of the day.

"Remember that the military is run, like anything else, by people. People are uncoordinated, lazy, foolish, and simple. I might want to please my captain but I don't know what's in his head, so I have to guess. If I guess wrong, I pay for it. That prevents me from taking chances. Also, being in the spotlight is exactly what they do *not* want. My best guess as to what's happening? At this point, they would have let the bulk of them go and would have tried to detain one or two as they left, hoping that those two simply slip through the cracks."

"That's... what if that was your mother or father?" she whispered, trying to stay unheard over the drone of the bus.

Taylor's jaw was set so hard she heard his teeth grind. "Really?" He blinked. "You think that hadn't occurred to me?" The anger in his eyes was frightening. "You think maybe there's a reason I've been a little distant? That maybe I have a hole drilling through my stomach because I'm worried about them and *I can't be there?*" He hissed the last part, choking down what sounded suspiciously like a scream.

The woman seated across the aisle from them shot him an uneasy glance, pulling her baby a little tighter into her arms.

Taylor's right hand clenched on his knee. The knuckles turned white.

Now that he was finally talking, everything came spilling out in an angry torrent of words.

"I should be there, next to Harold, taking on a tank with a shotgun. I should be helping everyone I've ever known as a child to slip away because *I* endangered them all, just like my brother accused me of doing. I should be cleaning up my own mistakes." He turned to her, his face set. Pale. His jaw set. "But I'm not. The reason I'm not is because I didn't leave you. *I never left you.* I'm here, now. We're taking the only course of action left... and if I'm a little distracted, maybe I have a damn good reason for it."

And just like that, Angelica's world came to a crashing halt for one horrifying moment. She tried to breathe and couldn't, suddenly realizing that she hadn't been in this alone.

But he had.

She reached to cover his hand with hers, but this time it was he who moved away. Her heart shattered.

"I'm sorry." The words seemed so frail and small when whispered. Like they couldn't begin to cover the multitude of sins she carried. "I've been... I try to... Taylor, you're the most important thing in the world to me." Tears splashed the back of her hands clasped in her lap. "I need you, and sometimes I forget that you need me. You're so... you. I really am sorry."

Taylor took a deep breath and reached over to cover her hand with his. "I pushed the exercises because it was something I knew, something I could..."

"Control?"

"Yeah. I can't stop Griselda—I can't even find her. I can't stop her from spreading info about us. I can't..." He looked down at his hand on hers. "I can't protect everyone. And I can't protect you from this... shit that madwoman did to you." He looked up at her, his eyes steely and his face set. "But I will never ever stop trying to protect you. I swear it."

Angelica lay her head on his shoulder, slowly, gently, this time giving him the time and option to push away. The muscles of his chest and in his shoulder felt solid, unyielding under his shirt. She placed a hand over his heart, just to feel it beat in his chest.

"This isn't your fault," she whispered into his shirt.

"Don't say that to Harold." She heard the low growl in the back of his throat.

She lifted her head to look at him for a moment and asked the question that she'd been avoiding. "What happened between the two of you?"

Taylor was quiet for so long that she wondered if maybe she'd pushed too hard after all. Maybe this truly wasn't any of her business. She bit her lip and waited him out.

"I left," he said finally, "to join the Marines. It wasn't a good idea, not really. The Marine Corps puts you through hell. They train you and burn away all the excess. Mentally and physically, they scrape you down until only the lean and efficient bits are left. Under that sort of strain and constant exhaustion, it's easy to shift accidently. Very easy. But I was so sure that I was above all that, that my control was so superior." He turned his head, staring out the window at the passing scenery as he spoke. "Two days before I shipped out, my brother took me out for a drink. That's what I thought, anyway. Turned out, he set me up. We hooked up with some friends, a few girls I thought were just friendly. But Harold had been setting this up for months."

Angelica didn't like where this was going. Harold seemed to need a good ass-kicking.

"We had way too much to drink, the bar we ended up at was a biker hangout, some words were exchanged, and we got into a fight. You know, a couple Minnesota farm boys in a bar fight, what could be more cliché, right? Except that one of the girls got hurt. It wasn't bad, but enough to enrage me. I get protective, if you haven't noticed. Anyway, I found out later that it didn't actually happen. Harold set the whole thing up."

Her head on his shoulder still, she stared at his reflection in the glass, understanding why he looked away, hiding the pain etched on his face. She closed her eyes, allowing him his privacy. "Why?" she asked when the story didn't seem forthcoming.

Taylor sighed. "To prove a point. He knows how protective I get, even with strangers. He was trying to get me riled enough that I would shift." Taylor's eyes focused on something in the distant past. "It kind of worked. I went into a frenzy and would have killed them. Or at least really hurt them. But Harold stopped me, seeing that I had gone too far. He confessed to orchestrating the whole thing. I stormed out on him, made my own way home."

"You didn't change?"

"I did." Taylor said with a harsh laugh. "That night when I saw Harold, we both changed. Right then and there. My dad came into the middle of us, swinging a baseball bat. Harold got a few good rakes in down Dad's back and legs, but that bat broke my shoulder and Harold's hip." He shrugged like it was nothing.

Angelica gasped, horrified. Remembering Nikki's slap across Taylor's face. The easy brutality in Harold's actions. Was this what it meant to be a tiger? Or any big cat?

But not Taylor. Taylor isn't like that. She dug her hand into his shirt, holding him tightly as though to keep him from harm. What was it like to grow up in such an environment? And how would it be when they found the elders?

What if Taylor kills because of how he was raised? Does he carry this violence, too?

Suddenly she was scared. More scared than she'd ever been. She had to forcibly remind herself that she'd never seen anything violent or abusive from him since they'd been together. But he also hadn't seemed surprised, or even shocked, by Nikki's slap.

"What happened next?" she asked through lips that seemed suddenly very dry.

"The bones mended as we changed back, but my father just stood there, blood streaming down his leg and arm, holding the bat like it was Excalibur. I begged him to shift, to heal, but he stared at me and gritted his teeth and said he wouldn't shift now if it meant his life. He was too ashamed of his sons and the curse that had been laid on them to even pretend it was okay. I'd never seen him so angry before in my life."

Angelica tried to picture the giant of man bloodied and holding a club, taking on two tigers in the bloom of their youth, and shuddered.

"He threw us both out. I was set to leave anyway, but Harold... he had to find his way for a year after that. He and Dad eventually reconciled, but he still hates me for it. It took me a little longer to come home again."

She nodded, so full of mixed feelings that she had no idea what to say anymore. "They're going to be okay, Taylor," she whispered, though right now she was having trouble forgiving any of them.

He reached up and cupped her cheek, pressing her head again to his shoulder. "I think the nightmare would be to lose him before I could..." He let the sentence go unfinished. "He attacked me through the only weakness he knew I had."

"Your protective instinct," Angelica whispered. "Like the way you're protecting me now."

"And failing."

"No." She lifted her head. "No, not that. I...I needed you to know what to do. I needed you to have the answers so that I didn't have to find them. I'm sorry about that. I know I'm unique. You don't know everything. You can't. But when I realized that, I got scared and lashed out because I still wanted you to fix things."

"We *will* find the answers," he said, kissing the top of her head. "Together."

They rode in silence, her head on his chest, feeling him breathe, feeling the warmth of him.

"So..." Angelica whispered in the silence of their trip. "Here we are. A tiger and a lion riding a Greyhound."

Taylor's laugh was the first one she'd heard since they'd returned from Africa.

IT SHOULDN'T HAVE BEEN a surprise, but there were no direct flights from Duluth to Nepal. The next flight available had them leave Duluth in an hour. That was the good news. The bad news was everything else that followed.

The flight went from Duluth to Chicago. From there the next stop was Beijing, and from there to Chengdu and then Lhasa and from there to Kathmandu. In all, it was a 41-hour journey. After *that*... well, Taylor hadn't broached it with her, but the biggest issue, assuming that their luck held and helicopters didn't descend out of a blue sky to snatch them away to secret laboratories, was where they would go once they arrived. SECRET COMPOUND OF ANCIENT SHAPESHIFTERS wasn't something you just looked up on Google maps.

And Taylor had no idea where it was. He could get as far as Kathmandu, but that was because whenever he'd asked before the elders in his community waved his questions off with a vague "Kathmandu" reply. It had been too long, too many years since anyone from Taylor's family had even had contact with the elders. It had been years, and by years they meant decades since anyone had ventured that far into the outside world.

With the exception of Taylor.

So, he had no idea how long it would take to find them from there. Or even how to go about doing it.

And yet, they possessed greater knowledge than any other shifter community. And if the one Taylor had grown up in was accomplished at staying hidden, he could only imagine how much more difficult it would be to find the elders.

He didn't say any of this. Angelica was quiet as he dropped nearly ten-grand for the two of them to get there and back. Her eyes widened at the amount, though she said nothing. Maybe the return ticket seemed optimistic, but he said he was going to believe in happy endings. She smiled a little at that. They sat and just breathed for a while at the airport with Angelica curled up on the seat beside him. He noted that her position was almost cat-like, but bit his tongue. The last thing he wanted to do now was nag her, especially now when they were both so much on edge. Even just getting this far had proved to be frustrating.

He stared at his hands. On the last leg of the bus trip, as they neared Duluth, some teens had boarded the bus. They'd been loud, brash, obnoxious. Taylor had been too tempting a target, it was a case of finding the fastest gun in town and calling them out the first day. Some words were exchanged, and at a rest stop they decided to stay for the next bus. In the men's room. At least, he was pretty sure they would wake in time for the next bus.

What surprised him was that the cat had been there for the fight. Instead of interfering and making him clumsy the cat instead integrated into the fight and his reaction time tripled, while his flexibility increased by a factor.

To his surprise, man and beast came to a tight-knit bond. With time to kill while waiting for their flight, he had time to think this through. And maybe very carefully experiment some with that.

The cat was simply pleased with himself in a way that only a cat could be.

There are advantages to having two legs and not four.

And there is reason that we use the expression "moved like a cat." That was... impressive.

It was.

As much as the cat took it in stride Taylor worried about this new relationship, like a dog trying to get marrow from a bone. This was the true power of the shift, the meld. The joining of the two had just taken on a new dimension unheard of by his own people. Forget fantasies of armies shifting and turning into tigers and charging the ranks of bullets and mortars. Think instead of men, fully realized, who could run, move, leap, and flow the way a cat did. Such an army would be irresistible, and impossible to defeat.

But Taylor had never met anyone before who could speak directly to his cat. You turned, you woke, and you tried to figure out what happened while you were gone. It was that way for everyone. The way it always had been.

Until he'd been able to change his eyesight while driving from the compound at night. And only his eyesight.

He'd blown that off with Angelica, acted like it was no big deal. But when it happened, it almost took him off the road that led to Augustine's barn. He'd driven in pitch blackness and was able to see as if it were noon on a cloudless day.

How did I do that?

You didn't. I did.

That was startling, too. The cat took the initiative? Changed *just* that much of him because he needed it? They were supposed to be two bodies in one, but now they were blending. Not just in body, but in mind.

Taylor was trying to come to terms with this new information, when he heard Angelica gasping beside him. He turned and looked at her. Her eyes were wide with fear and she was staring at the television in the corner, the one with...

Taylor exhaled as if he'd just been hit.

On the news bulletin interrupting the courtship between Nancy and Thomas, even though Nancy knew he was the father of Linda's child, who turned out to be a space alien—the news reader seemed confused and intent. The scrawl line under his face read, LION SPOTTED IN PILLAGE MN. From there it cut to a frantic woman who was gesturing with one hand, clutching a barking terrier to her chest with the other. The dog seemed hell-bent on attacking the microphone thrust in her mistress's face. The sound was off, so Taylor couldn't hear what was being said, but her caption was EYEWITNESS TO LION ATTACK. As the woman finished her sentence, the dog squirmed and fell from her grasp.

The newsreader returned, said something else, and then the television switched to a distorted, grainy view that the caption identified as COURTESY OF PILLAGE BANK. In the picture, a lioness walked in front of the ATM. Worse, she actually looked up *into* the camera and licked her lips before loping off-camera.

Isn't she magnificent?

A pencil sketch of Taylor followed that image, bearing the identification of PERSON OF INTEREST, and the name JAMES SUMMERS.

Taylor bent low at the waist and threaded his fingers behind his neck as if he were stretching. More like hiding. He stayed that way until Angelica whispered, "It's over."

"I need to get out of here."

He stood and walked to the waiting area of a neighboring gate. Angelica followed him.

"Where did they get that image of you?" she hissed.

"Probably from that sheriff," Taylor said out of the corner of his mouth. An idea occurred to him as he tried to *not* look around the gate. He fished in his wallet and pulled out a twenty. He handed her the cash and pretended to be very interested in a flyer he found for the treatment of stomach ulcers. "Do me a favor, go to that little store and see if they have any little makeup mirrors."

She pocketed the cash, her face so pale it was a wonder she wasn't attracting attention just for that. He hated putting her through this, to make her walk away alone like that right now. But she proved she still had that inner spark when her chin came up, proud and determined, and she asked, "What do you have planned?"

Good girl.

"Something. I don't know if I can do it or not." It wasn't a very satisfying answer, but she accepted it all the same and turned to go, looking not so much frightened as determined.

I think I can do what you're thinking.

He studied the flyer, looking over every inch of it twice, and was halfway through a third pass of it when she returned. She handed him a small grooming kit, complete with tiny mirror. He pocketed the item and headed for the men's room.

The first stall he came to wasn't one he wanted to stay in any longer than it took to back out and try not to gag. The one two down from that left a comfortable buffer between him and the first and was relatively clean. Thankful to be out of sight, he latched the door.

Are you sure about this?

No.

He held the mirror up and let the cat move.

It was a strange process. It felt incredible. Somewhat painful and more just weird. The nose flattened and shifted. It was too much, and he pulled back by concentrating on where he wanted it to be. The jaw rippled, and though it changed its shape it looked—melted. His brow jutted and his eyebrows lightened.

It's a different face but the jaw looks unnatural. I can't go out like this.

The cat moved again and thick, tawny hair jutted from his skin around the jaw and over the upper lip.

The lip is split.

In response, the hair over the upper lip grew longer. Taylor was now a man who might have been a pugilist and taken one too many blows to the face. With the full beard, though, it didn't match the hair on his head. The man looking back at him in the mirror was a complete stranger.

Wow. That's just... wow. Can you hold it?

I thought you were.

He looked again and sighed as a commotion outside in the men's room drew his attention. He stood, took a breath, and unlatched the door. He turned quickly and flushed to complete the illusion of having been in there for other reasons. A very nervous-looking security guard and two policemen looked at him as he left the stall and ignored him. One of the policemen had the sketch of Taylor in his hand.

Taylor washed his hands and left the restroom. Angelica stood outside, anxiously trying to see past him into the bathroom. He walked past her and returned to their original seat. The police came back out, the security guard shaking his head and looking miffed.

They went to Angelica and showed her the picture. She shook her head no. The police gave the security guard a long look and he vehemently said something Taylor couldn't hear. When they left, Angelica was still looking at the bathroom, but her expression was one of complete confusion.

Taylor picked up his bag and set it in the seat beside him, closest to her. It took a moment, but she noticed it finally and went to sit behind him.

"Taylor?" She had her gaze focused on a magazine she'd found discarded on a nearby seat, staring at it intently, keeping it raised enough so observers wouldn't see her lips move. He smiled a little, pleased that she was still thinking despite what had to be a terrifying moment for her.

"Yep." He spoke the word softly, stretching and staring across the way at the board that displayed departure times.

"How?"

"I don't really know. Just pretend you don't know me and get on the plane alone."

"But won't they know your seat number?"

He shook his head. He hoped not. He'd bought the tickets under a different name. The phony passport in his pocket would hold up to decent scrutiny. So would Angelica's. At least he hoped so. "All they know is one excited guard thought he saw someone. They have no reason to believe him. Not now."

She was quiet a moment. Then, so softly he almost didn't hear, she said, "*That* exercise I want to learn." Her tone was wistful.

He smiled.

That's my girl.

But I do not think I want her to have a beard.

Chapter 13

Angelica spent the entire time on the tarmac holding her breath. She was certain that at any moment the police would bust down the ramp and drag them out of the plane. And no matter how many cell phones there were to record it, she was sure that they could be "disappeared." What they were was just that important to the government. *Any* government. She was starting to understand why Taylor's people never left the north woods of Minnesota.

And also starting to understand what it cost them to leave there now.

In the meantime, she did the only thing she could: she maintained the illusion that she didn't know Taylor. Which was fast becoming more and more far-fetched. She'd been snuggling next to him on the seat for the last twenty minutes. And though he no longer looked the same, the fact that she was in the seat for "Mrs. Summer" while he was seated in the seat for "Mr. Summer" seemed a little too obvious at best.

Come to think of it, that name was stupid enough for them to both be arrested as too damn clumsy to be spies. While they waited to take off, Taylor busied himself in a Sky Mall magazine and she tried to count the repetitions of a pattern on the seat in front of her. Finally, they were airborne and the odyssey to Nepal had started. There was no going back. Not that she wanted to. She couldn't get her head around someone recognizing Taylor from a small town to a nation-wide search. It made absolutely no sense—unless, of course, the government was involved.

"So... how?" she asked as soon as they were safely airborne. She'd been trying to play it cool, but she was no longer able to contain her curiosity.

"I...I'm not sure."

I did it.

"It was a collaborative effort."

"I thought..." Angelica looked around and whispered, "I thought you said that there's no direct communication between you and the cat."

"There isn't. I mean, there wasn't. I-I can't explain it, but whatever that doctor did to me I've been actually talking to him and him to me ever since."

"What?" Angelica stared at him. "You mean like hearing voices?"

He shot her a sideways look. "I recognize that look. Don't go diagnosing me. Remember, a couple of months ago you would have locked away anyone who said they could shift."

"Fair point." She took his hand and held it for a while, even if her brain was still trying to catalogue different mental disorders that would result in hearing voices. "So, um," she tried to stifle a giggle, "how long are you keeping that face?"

"Well, we have a stop in Chicago. From there, the next stop is China. Once we're safely out of the States, I guess."

"I like the old you."

"To be honest, it kind of aches. It actually hurts holding it in this shape."

She looked at him thoughtfully, studying the way his eyebrows formed, the slope of the nose. "Does this mean I can do that, too?"

Taylor stared at her for a moment. "I'm not even sure how I am. This..." he indicated his face, "this isn't normal. Hell, being able to communicate with the cat isn't normal."

Angelica started. "Wait, what? I thought those exercises—"

"I don't know what my mother told you, but I had you do them because I did. Because my friends did. Because Harold did. All I know is that I haven't heard of anyone who actually..." he thought around for the word, "coexists with their inner cat."

Only inner when you're on two legs. When we're free, you're the inner.

"I think I'm the only one to *ever* do this. It's... I don't know what it is."

"Are you—I mean, did Melinda damage you?" It was a new thought. She hadn't realized that he'd changed, too. That he'd been struggling with a body he didn't understand as much as she was.

Why didn't he tell me sooner? She snorted quietly. *Probably because I never bothered to ask.*

"I feel fine," Taylor said, waving off her concern. "It's not like there's a blood test to determine if there's an issue with my inner cat."

Maybe not, but he didn't exactly need to snap at her like that. Angelica nodded and sat back. There was something he wasn't saying, that much she could tell. What it was, now, that was another question. But he was closed off, and her attempts at questioning him were only shutting him down further. His family, the whole thing with his brother—how could she know what he was feeling? It was like being in love with a rock or an iron statue. The worse things got, the less he said.

With a sigh she curled up as comfortably as she could against the window, her face pressed against the glass. Thankfully it was a short flight to Chicago. In no time at all, they were descending.

There was a plane change in O'Hare. It was an entire airline change. They had to proceed to a different terminal, a journey of some distance. There was little time to talk as they found a shuttle train that circumvented the terminal and headed out to the international terminal. And when they finally got aboard the shuttle, the crowds were pressed in too close to talk about anything real. At least no one was looking for them.

"This is like an enclosed little city," she said as the train sped silently on the edge of the building. Taylor had told her to wait before they boarded. He'd disappeared and then came back shortly. "Shops, restaurants." She glanced over at him. "I didn't see what you got. Don't tell me—you have a secret craving for Necco wafers that I didn't know about." Angelica kept her tone light. Teasing. The tension from their earlier conversation had followed them off the plane and she was desperate for a fresh start, for him to look at her the way he had in Africa, or South America. To become *him* again.

To her surprise, Taylor held up a book. It was a mystery/spy novel that boasted *First Time in Paperback* on the cover and had a half-dozen recommendations from people she'd never heard of on the back.

"Seriously? A spy novel?"

Taylor grinned, and for a moment she caught sight of his old self. "I get addicted to them. I can't help it. Besides, this next flight is going to be 20 solid hours."

"Really?" Angelica sighed. She plucked the book from his hand, wishing she'd had the foresight to find reading material. "What's it about?"

The train separated from the building and headed silently out on its own. It glided into the setting sun and she watched the shadows lengthen and deepen, listening to Taylor talk about his favorite authors and characters. She had no idea what a Reacher was or what Ian Fleming had to do with James Bond, but she didn't care. This was peace finally. Angelica rested her head on his shoulder, and felt the low rumble in Taylor's chest as he spoke with a soft satisfaction that brought a silent ache to her heart.

Please let this moment go on forever. It's a good one. We're safe right now.

O'Hare's international terminal was far less busy than the main terminal. It was calmer somehow, maybe even cleaner. Angelica disembarked from the train, holding her breath. But no uniformed figures waited to intercept them on the way to the terminal. The people milling around didn't carry fliers with Taylor's picture. She supposed the goings-on in a small town in deep-woods Minnesota didn't much affect them. With some relief Taylor excused himself and went into the restroom, only to emerge a few minutes later 'clean-shaven'. His face had resumed its shape and he looked younger somehow, more alive.

More him.

She stroked his cheek with approval and kissed him for good measure.

The wait for this flight was uneventful. Angelica tried to search the internet for news coming out of Minnesota, hoping to glean some information about Taylor's family. The media silence was unnerving. Apparently, the breaking news was limited to local coverage and wasn't the big item she thought it might have been. Should have been.

Someone's suppressed it. Someone with the power to suppress it.

The thought put a knot of fear in her belly that stayed with her all the way across continents and oceans. It followed her into her dreams when she finally slept, safely ensconced in what turned out to be a first-class pod, thirty-five-thousand feet above the rest of the world.

THE CROSS-PACIFIC FLIGHT went by without a hitch. Almost no shifting, no fighting, and actually some sleeping. Somehow Angela managed to relax and not send anyone screaming "LION!" as they raced down the aisle.

Beijing was incredibly crowded, and Angelica still wasn't sure they'd gotten on the correct connecting flight until after they'd landed. A lot of pantomime and gestures and pointing to the ticket stub seemed to be the correct procedure. Taylor towered over the local populace, making him stick out like a sore thumb. Angelica let her dark hair hang forward, around her face, and tried desperately to blend into the woodwork. She didn't feel safe until she was on the plane, and even then wasn't able to shake the anxiety that crowded out her every thought.

By now, they had to have been spotted somewhere. Reported to someone. It was a paranoid, crazy thought, but the longer they were out in the open the larger the risk. Add to that the stress of worrying about changing where someone would see, and she was jumping out of her skin. Literally.

Only once on the plane had Taylor had to wake her abruptly. Traveling first class helped, she was sure. The flight attendants were used to employing discretion toward their first class passengers, and the light blanket she'd covered herself with before falling asleep had kept the fur safely out of sight, until she'd gotten herself back under control.

The flight out of Shanghai offered no such privacy. After some discussion, Angelica resolved to not sleep until they safely arrived. By the time they landed in Chengdu, she was sure it was a moot point anyway; there was no way she could relax enough to sleep regardless of whether she actually wanted to or not.

Thankfully the Chengdu and Lhasa airports were smaller, less frenetic. It was easier to find the connecting flights there, even if that was largely due to the ability to make fewer wrong choices. It was during the final approach to the airport in Kathmandu when she raised the question that had been bothering her since they'd left Minnesota.

"Taylor? What happens when we get there? I mean, from the airport, where do we go?"

Taylor shrugged without looking up from his book. "I don't know."

"What?"

He put his finger between the pages to mark his place and glanced over at her. "We broke off from them hundreds of years ago. No one is still alive from those days to ask. Hence, no one knows where they are."

She looked out the window at the mountains that seemed far too close to the runway. The ground rose up to meet the plane; the city spread out around them, much larger than she'd anticipated. Kathmandu had felt like it was on the furthest edges of the world, but she could have sworn she'd just seen a sign for KFC. The whole experience was surreal. It had been two full days, 42 hours in airplanes, and she was gritty and dirty and felt like she was marinating in her own sweat. Yet the snow was heavy on the mountains, and somewhere out there was Everest, the tallest mountain in the world.

And a jungle. Two days ago she had no idea Nepal even had a jungle, where big cats roamed.

She looked back at him. "Please tell me you're joking."

He shook his head.

"Taylor... why... what was the point..."

"Because," he said simply, setting the book down in his lap, "in my entire life my mother has never hit me. Ever. This was a first. I have never seen her this way. My dad? Maybe. But for her to lose her cool like that tells me that something is deeply wrong. If you only knew her..." He looked at her with sad eyes. "It felt like I didn't know her at all."

Angelica stared at her hands, bunched in the sweater she'd taken off when the flight had gotten warm and had somehow wound up wadded up on her lap. "Then why? Why would she hit you now?"

Taylor glanced at her. "Maybe because my mom needed to get it through my head that you're the important one. I needed to see you through this and I wasn't listening."

"You were looking for support," she said, and winced a little as the plane touched the tarmac and promptly bounced a little more roughly than necessary. "And I was too upset about my prognosis."

"So was my mother. Not for the same reason, I think. See... we're...we're not doing well—as a species, I mean. There aren't a lot of us, and though the shift gene is dominant in our children it's less and less so every time someone marries a non-shifter. And to tell the truth, there aren't a lot of non-shifters who would welcome sharing their lives with one. Our children..." He grinned. "...have special needs."

"At puberty," she reminded him with a wry shake of her head. "That *has* to make things easier."

"Yes, puberty and easy are two contradicting words, aren't they? But as children we have to be very careful because we have the advantage to 'my dad can beat up your dad', but we can't say anything to outsiders. Sometimes we do anyway."

"Yikes."

"The thing is..." He spoke over the announcements. They were in Chinese and Nepali anyway, and without gesturing and pointing to a ticket there was no chance to understand any of it. "...those who do marry—sometimes the cat gets lonely. They have no mate..."

She IS my mate. Even before.

"I mean no mate they can run with and be a cat with. And sometimes the spouses become resentful because they don't have the physical benefits, like instant healing and a longer life."

"So, I represent..."

"The continuation of our species. If we can stabilize you, we can offer it to others and *maybe* we can get new blood into the group. Before we start to inbreed."

It was an uncomfortable thought. Going from being an oddity to the possible salvation of a species in ten minutes would leave anyone unsettled. Angelica couldn't wrap her mind around it. What would their children be? Lions? Tigers? Ligers? Oh, my...

She gathered her belongings and followed Taylor out of the airplane in something of a daze. The air was thin from the higher elevation, but dry. Taylor had assured her there were forests here as thick as the Amazon, only a bright, brilliant green, but all she could see was open land covered in industrial buildings and the occasional pagoda-styled apartment building—and in the distance, those amazing snow-capped mountains.

They truly were at the top of the world.

The airport felt dark and old after having been in so many airports that were much more modern. It was just as crowded. The people hurried past in a chatter of unfamiliar languages. Finding their way was something of a challenge, though thankfully there were a handful of signs in English to guide them. Even better, they had only to deal with customs, having carried their two bags with them and not having to try to figure out the baggage claim.

Outside they stood a moment and stared at the sea of white cars and vans that were taxis, disoriented by the sheer cacophony of noise that greeted them. Here the cars honked and swerved like so many prima ballerinas, each pushing the other out of the spotlight and dancing to different music.

Angelica looked around her. Near the entrance was a large Buddha, reminding her that this was another world entirely. Fascinated, she started taking in the details that she'd missed in their haste to find their way outside. The people, for example, were fascinating. For the most part, they were short and rather squat. There was a definite Mongolian influence, though there was a great deal of Chinese as well. The contrast in looking at Taylor was remarkable. She saw only his Viking heritage. He stood a good head taller than the tallest native and his build was Nordic. He stood on the sidewalk, trying to talk to a pair of men she guessed were drivers of the taxis. They smiled and bowed and offered to take them to the line of hotels that were easily visible.

One of these things is not like the other...

"So, if your people came from here," she said when he joined her, shaking his head, "they weren't native, were they?"

"Actually, they arrived here in long-ships from Scandinavia," a large, barrel-chested man with a ready smile and a thick mane of grey both on his head and on his chin interrupted them.

Angelica started in surprise, as she hadn't seen him come up. Taylor jumped back, wary, his hand going reflexively to the small of his back, though Angelica knew he had no weapon there.

The man clapped Taylor on the shoulder and gave a hearty laugh. "Relax, old man, they're hardly going to take you out in the middle of a crowd." He ushered them toward the street. "Taylor, Angelica, I'd like to welcome you. I hope you won't be put out by my rushing you, but I do have a car waiting. If you'll come this way, please."

Chapter 14

"Who are you?" Angelica asked.

Taylor shook his head to warn her. You didn't ask questions. Not yet anyway. "It's okay." That was all he was able to get out before they were rushed into the waiting car. Even then, no conversation ensued. Just silence.

The drive seemed to take forever. Several times Angelica opened her mouth to say something, and each time Taylor shook his head and she'd close her mouth. It took several hours to get to the compound. Rather than head toward the mountains they traveled through the heart of the city, eventually going south and then east. Initially they passed through the tourist areas. Angelica stared out the window and Taylor followed her gaze, seeing fine restaurants side by side with places that would supply you for a trek up Everest. He realized that he'd forgotten that climbing the world's tallest mountain was a deadly game for the rich to play at, and it showed in the luxurious storefronts and hotels.

Soon enough the roads found neighborhood streets, and the houses took on a distinctly foreign look. Shrines were a constant, as were pagodas and other architecture that reminded her that this was an area rich in history. Finally, this old sector of town gave way to an industrial park. They passed warehouses and factories that belched smoke into a sky already hazy with smog that rose only so far, and was trapped in the valley by the mountains around them.

While the roads started well, by the time they left the city behind and wound down into the ever-thickening green of the jungle Taylor could see Angelica's spine was a line of flame up her back. Their host apologized profusely for the condition of the road, but said little else other than, "The elders will answer all your questions."

They arrived in the darkness, spent and exhausted. They were shown to a small building that looked like a mud-daubed hut on the outside, but was a nice little room with wooden planks for walls and floor of terracotta tiles on the inside. Outside, the world had taken on the darkness that comes of being surrounded by a thick and verdant jungle. Oddly enough, after so much time in the Amazon and later Africa, it was this that allowed Angelica to relax. Taylor could see it in her posture and on her face. For the past two years the jungle had been her home in one incarnation or another, and while this was a new place to her, at the same time it wasn't.

With the cessation of the panic that had engulfed them for too many days and far more miles than they could count, Angelica saw nothing in the room besides the giant bed and collapsed across it without removing any of her clothes. She was done, plain and simple. With a relief that bordered on the orgasmic, she finally slept.

Well, that didn't take long. Taylor stood and looked at Angelica, his face softening. It had been a hellish amount of travel in a handful of days, and she'd withstood the strain well. He studied her pale face, the way she curled around the pillows, and for a long moment wanted nothing more than to hold her in his arms and kiss away the frown that followed her even into sleep.

Instead, he did the only thing he could do. He slipped the shoes from her feet. He loosened her belt and opened her jeans in case she shifted, so that she might slip easily from the clothes. She murmured in her sleep but didn't wake as he removed her shirt and bra, which only went to show just how utterly exhausted she was. Realizing that she wasn't going to wake anytime soon, he thought about it a moment and finished the job, pulling her jeans down and draping them over green chair tucked into the corner of the room.

She stirred only a little in all of it.

Poor girl.

With a wary eye on her, lest she shift suddenly in her sleep, he stripped and settled next to her. Immediately she moved toward him, nestling into his arms so naturally that it felt as though she were designed to fit just there. He kissed her shoulder and pulled the single sheet over her and then himself. It was too hot for more than that thin material. He lay there, his arm around her, looking at her hair in the moonlight that filtered through the window screen.

Then he blinked and it was morning. He had no memory of falling asleep, of being aware of anything in the night at all.

For a moment he panicked. What if she'd changed in her sleep and he had been too tired to notice? But she was still in the same place, and even the same position, curled into a little ball next to him. He tried to move and discovered how stiff he was.

He chuckled when he discovered that it wasn't just his muscles that were stiff.

He looked at her and sighed. She was completely wiped out by the journey, and still slept though her cheeks had gained some color and were delicately flushed now. Her lips parted as she breathed, long and slow. No, he wasn't about to wake her just because his body was wanting attention. He tucked himself around her as best he could and draped an arm over her, letting the erection press against her, in case she should wake up enough to notice and might actually want a little of that kind of attention herself.

Taylor could be very optimistic sometimes.

But sleep eluded him as much as release. He'd been worn out enough that his body had shut down when he lay down, but now that it had its rest, though he could tell it was still not enough after so many days of adrenaline-fueled panic, the worries that plagued him kept him awake and anxious.

Angelica seemed likewise on edge. She moaned in the throes of a dream and shifted slightly against his hardness, automatically adjusting to stay in a somewhat comfortable position. It wasn't easy. He didn't remember taking off her underwear last night, but one of them must have; she was naked under the sheet just like he was.

His hand held her arms, but he felt a nipple touching his forearm as she breathed. Her back was a perfect line from neck to hips. *The most perfect line is the line of a woman's back,* he thought, recalling an old essay he'd read in college called "The Line of Beauty".

But as the lioness, it's even nicer.

She turned her head and partially opened one eye to look at him. "Are you happy to see me?" she asked in a thick voice, but that smile was all lust.

He flexed a muscle and she giggled.

"Yeah. I think you are." She turned and groaned as muscles had to suddenly break the position she'd been in for far too long. "I need to find a bathroom," she said, rolling over to kiss him. "And I should wash up a little."

He watched her get up and walk to the door across from the entrance they'd come through. Whatever this place was it was nicely constructed, with wooden planks that had a patina, the sort of weathering that old barns in the Midwest would get after years of exposure to the elements. The walls were planed and sanded and the slats were set close enough that they sealed the place without using any sort of filler, somewhat like the interior of a log cabin, but somewhat not. This felt older. Even European in feel.

That was all taken in a secondary view from the side of his vision. A different vision was forefront in his mind. It didn't help his aroused state that a beautiful naked woman was striding across the room and headed to an unknown door. He watched her pad over the hardwood floors and open the door with a certain appreciation for the beautiful woman she was. He wasn't sure who jumped more when she squealed and jumped back, slamming it shut.

Taylor was up in an instant. Angelica, though, just stood there and laughed, one hand on her hip, hair cascading down in a tangled curtain that she pushed out of her face with the other. "Just kidding." She grinned mischievously and her gaze fell to his waist. "Why should you be the only one who gets a good view?" She was still laughing when the pillow hit her chest. She caught it and lobbed it back, narrowly missing his head.

"Come and check this out!" she said, as thrilled as a little girl as she threw open the door and stood back to let him see past her. The door opened to a large bathroom complete with toilet, bidet, and a large tub. The tub seemed to be a single piece of wood that was carved out and sealed. It was gorgeous, gleaming in the light from the open window.

"Just enough room for two," she said, her eyes sparkling as she reached for him, grabbing the part of him that was currently the most predominant and giving him a tug, then got a funny look on her face. She glanced at the toilet, then at him, her face turning redder by the minute. He stifled a laughed as she let go and stepped backwards into the bathroom, holding up one finger to indicate that he needed to wait.

Only when he heard the water running in the tub did she open the door. Now it was his turn to shoo her out. "Um... between you and the running water, I'm fairly desperate..."

"Aren't we the romantic pair?" she laughed, and stepped back into the bedroom to give him an equal moment of privacy.

The bathroom was a beautiful thing, built along the same lines as the rest of the place, but the fixtures gleamed in the early morning sunlight. It wasn't what he'd expected by a long shot and he wondered what it said about the people who lived here, a little luxury in the middle of nowhere.

He finished and went to check the tub. The water was quite hot, hotter than he'd expected. The door opened and Angelica came in, holding a small box. "I found a little gift basket," she said, holding up a small wooden box that held a handwritten note, reading, "For the bath."

She opened it and took a cautious sniff and then took a deep breath. "Oh... it's... heavenly."

She handed it to Taylor, who took a sniff.

Is that what catnip is like? I've always wanted to try catnip...

Taylor didn't need the cat to finish the thought. It wasn't relaxing—it was hypnotic and brought back the erection that he'd lost to morning ritual. In fact, it not only brought him back to life but it made his erection throb. "This is formulated to the cat..." he murmured, his voice thick. He was having difficulty forming words "...to the inner cat... it's kind of an aphrodisiac..."

"I'll say." Angelica was looking pointedly at his loins. Without giving himself the time to consider the consequences fully, he upended the box into the tub and the resulting aroma filled the bathroom instantly.

Oh, yeah, that was good.

For her, too, apparently. An instant later she was there in his arms, arms and legs wrapped around him, her mouth devouring his in a series of passionate kisses that left him gasping for air.

He picked her up and stepped into the tub with her. She giggled as he settled her between his legs. She raised herself up a little to allow him to slide under her to a more comfortable position, and then slowly settled on his hardness, allowing him to fill her as she forced herself down around him, with no preamble, no foreplay at all.

He growled and bit her ear. She screamed, a sound half-animal in passion as she rose and fell on him, maybe a little carefully at first. Then with more confidence as the water echoed the sounds of their love, lapping at the rim of the tub and sending cascades of water over the edge.

He reached from behind, liking the way she was turned away from him, as it allowed him to hold her breasts, soapy thumbs rubbing her nipples and teasing her breasts. She clamped down on him, pulling him further inside her, milking his hardness.

He groaned and ran his hands down her slick flesh, sitting up to reach between her legs and caress her as he slid in and out of her warmth. Her passion ignited his and he felt himself near the edge.

She rocked back in his grasp and he felt the first wave of her orgasm hit. It pulsed against him and triggered his own. His release was nearly blinding, intense and severe. It tore through him and poured out into her and he shuddered in the throes of it, his legs shaking and his eyes clamped shut.

He fell back against the tub and she collapsed on top of him, shuddering with him as the aftershocks rolled through her again and again.

"Whatever that is..." He swallowed, still stunned by the violence of their passion and the speed with which the whole thing was over. He tried to clear his throat and began again. "Whatever that is, I want some to go..."

She nodded, breathing heavily against him. Her could feel the thunder of her heart beneath his palm. She felt down between her legs and whispered in awed wonder, "You're staying hard."

Painfully so. "Yeah."

She nodded and took a deep breath, twisting to look him in the eye. "Well, by all means, let's not waste it..."

"I DON'T KNOW WHAT THAT was," Angelica said as they collapsed on the bed, still dripping but too tired to care enough to towel off, "but I really liked it."

Taylor pulled her close, but his gaze was distant as he turned things over in his mind. Angelica waited him out, recognizing his need to think things through his way. Besides, being curled next to him with her head on his shoulder was pleasant enough by itself, especially with his skin still tainted with the soft scent of the bath.

Delightful. She was practically purring.

Maybe he was, too. He certainly seemed content as he spoke, one hand making lazy circles around her breast. "So," he paused to kiss the top of her head as he shifted her a little until her head was just there, in that hollow of his shoulder that seemed to have been created to cradle her head just so. "An evil scientist hacked up some cooked pheromones and suddenly I have a skull full of cat, and now these elders have cobbled some feline sex smell? How much of a cat is in their nose?"

It was a good question, and one she'd been wondering for some time now. "I don't know, I didn't really study veterinary medicine at all. I tried to search out some articles on cats and pheromones after that mess in Africa, but we've been so busy I haven't really had time to go all that deeply into them. I think it's probably quite a bit."

"That much I could tell without articles," he chuckled.

"But smelling cancer, that's a new one," she said, remembering the woman in the diner and hoping that she'd gone to her doctor like she'd advised her to. "Is that something you could always do?"

"Not directly." He pulled her closer, not that it was possible, but she recognized the gesture for what it was, the need to feel as intimate and as entwined as the sheets that tangled around their still damp bodies. Under the heat of the day the windows were open, and the ceiling fan rotated with infinite slowness over their naked forms. "The first time it happened, it was with a horse. Horses don't much like large predatory animals—they're a good source of protein, but if you introduce the cat while the horse is young they do eventually get used to it, which is why you saw some horses out at my parents' farm. Anyway, there was a kid, too young to change yet that I was watching her for her parents. She wanted to go riding and I loped along beside her, or at least I said I would and I was told that I did. But when I switched back I knew that horse was sick. I didn't even think about it, like it was a mare, it had four legs and cancer, and it never occurred to me that I shouldn't know that. So when the cat smells it the result, not the smell, stays in the memory."

"And now? Now that you're connected?"

"Now I smelled it, too. It took me a minute to figure out." He paused and shrugged. "And then he just told me," he said, rolling his eyes.

"You're talking to him now, aren't you?" She perked up and looked at him. He nodded. "Was he present while we..." She gestured to his naked body.

Taylor shrugged. "It's his body, too. And you're his mate, too."

She glanced up sharply. He'd mentioned that once before, but things had been so hectic then that she'd never really thought through the ramifications. "I'm what?" she asked, wanting clarification more than anything.

"Remember? You're his mate. He decided that before we did. In the Amazon. He decided that you were his mate."

Which really didn't tell her anything new at all. "I...I'm still not sure how to take that."

He laughed. "It's a compliment. Remember I said that often we marry non-shifters? If the inner cat..." his eyes took on that distant look for a split second he got when talking to the cat, "if the cat who is inner while in human form," he continued patiently, "doesn't like the spouse, it can be a problem."

"So... if...if two shifters marry do the cats... have sex?"

Taylor laughed. "Sorry, it wasn't the question that made me laugh, it was the loud, resounding YES that echoed in my head just now." He nodded slowly. "Yes, but it has to be done in a very controlled manner."

Her eyes widened. This was something she hadn't considered before. "What do you mean?"

"When a woman gets pregnant, there's a point where her body is a host to the baby and it's not able to be shoved aside with the organs and bones. No shifter changes during the last trimester of pregnancy. Besides, we don't know what would happen to the child if she did."

"And if she happens to get pregnant as a cat?"

"Same problem, with a bit of a complication."

"What 'complication'?"

"Six to eight children at once."

Angelica gasped and sat up. "Holy..." She looked down at herself and had this insane urge to clean herself out and fast. Taylor smiled and pulled her down again. "It's only if you mate as a cat. We haven't."

Still, their lack of birth control took on much higher proportions. Maybe rather than trusting birth control pills like she had been, she needed to consider other options as well. Just as a precaution. For now.

But what about someday? Do I want children with Taylor? She'd never seriously considered the question before. It wasn't a terrible idea. Just something she wasn't ready for.

"Sorry, just panicked a little." She lay back on him and sighed. "Taylor, can I ask you about—"

Unfortunately, their conversation was cut short by a polite knock on the door. "Please join us for lunch."

The timing was terrible, but what could she say? "We'll be right there. Thank you!" she called to the door, and twisted in his arms to kiss his pectoral. For a long moment she gazed into his eyes, seeing the disappointment mirrored there that was fast crowding out lust. Time to rejoin the world after all. She sat up and looked for her bag.

"Remember the nice man said he would take our bags for us?" Taylor asked, sitting up on the edge of the bed. "He never said *where* he would take them. They're not here."

Angelica stared at the floor, as though the bags would materialize somehow if she just looked at it hard enough. "What about the clothes we were wearing?"

"Apparently them, too. We were both so exhausted from the trip..." He must have seen her growing panic for he stopped talking and shook his head. "No, I undressed you. I undressed us both. When we went to sleep it was under the sheet. Someone came in here, took our clothes, and slipped out again. In complete darkness."

"So we're supposed to go to lunch naked?" Angelica asked, with a pained glance down at herself. While she had always been fairly comfortable in her own skin, this was certainly taking things to a different level. She stared him down, hands on her hips. "I parade you out there like that and every female under 80 is going to chase you down."

"What about the ones over 80?"

"They have walkers, so no chance of catching you," she said, throwing her hands in the air.

"There's a dresser," Taylor said, rising from the bed. He pulled open a drawer and removed a white bundle that looked soft. He shook it out. It was a cross between a karate gi and bathrobe. The pants were elastic at the waist and loose. If the person wearing them changed it would stretch as needed, and the durable material would stand up to anything but a direct assault from claws.

The top was a wrap-around with a belt that adjusted, and a quick-release on the belt to free it if the wearer shifted. She shook it out, somewhat dubious, but thought it might cover her modestly enough. The fabric was thin and porous enough to handle the heat, and most of all they were clean.

He took the shirt from her and held it against himself. His was also five sizes too small.

"I guess I'll have to tie it around my waist," he said, taking the sleeves and holding the material outstretched. "What do you think, front or back?" He demonstrated each possibility, each one worse than the last.

Angelica laughed despite herself and slid into the pants. "I think these are mine, doofus. Check that other drawer."

"'Doofus'? Is that like 'Honey'? Or 'Sweetheart'? I'm not sure I like it." He produced a duplicate set of clothing and shook them out.

"Taylor," Angelica said slowly as she tied the shirt on and twisted to see herself in the mirror. "They knew we were coming... that was weird enough. But how did they know our sizes?"

Taylor stopped with one leg in the pants. His eyes unfocused for a moment. "I think the cat just got chills."

"I don't know," she said, tightening the belt around the front and smoothing the fabric with a hand that shook just the littlest bit. "Something that can scare a tiger? Maybe we need to be on our guard here."

Taylor finished dressing. "At this point," he confessed, "I don't even know where we are in relation to Kathmandu, to the airport—to the rest of the world. I think that whatever they intend they're going to do no matter what we do."

She bit her lip and looked at him. "Was coming here a good idea?"

He took her in his arms and leaned her into his chest. "If what my mother said was true, even partly, then getting you here was and is worth all of this."

"Because I represent the survival of the species," she said. Her laugh was a little rueful, and maybe even a little hurt.

He held her at arm's length and looked into her eyes. "No. Because you represent the survival of my soul."

It was when he said things like that that she felt her insides melt, just like all those sappy heroines did in those torrid romance novels she used to devour on the sly. She opened her mouth to say something, though she knew full well that she'd never be able to come up with something half so poetic or even romantic, when she was saved by an interruption of a very hungry stomach making its needs known. So loud was the gurgle that erupted from her midsection that she snapped her mouth shut and felt the heat of a royal blush come on.

Taylor laughed and offered her his arm. "Let's go to lunch," he said, and just like that the moment was past. But there was a closeness between them, a comradery, that had been missing for far too long.

And so it was that she leaned on the strong muscular arm, and for the first time in forever felt cozy and protected. It was a lovely feeling even if it wasn't politically correct.

Maybe she was beyond political correctness for a little while.

Chapter 15

Angelica had lost track of time. She knew it was the middle of the day where they were. One, because they'd been told to join for lunch. Two, the sun beat down on them in the clearing. Around them the jungle glowed with an effervescent light that came down diffused through leaf and tree, but somehow still managed to cast a bright glow over everything. The day was warm, but it wasn't with the oppressive dense heat of the Amazon, or the sultry heat of Africa. This was more austere, if that was the right word. Here was an indifferent heat, one that wasn't trying to kill or disable. The heat here was indifferent, as if it didn't care about men one way or another.

As far as jungle, they certainly had that. Angelica had always pictured Nepal, when she'd pictured it at all, as being arid and windswept. Maybe with high mountain peaks, with Sherpas wearing thick parkas as they guided tourists up Everest. This place, though, was obviously somewhere in the lower elevations. Here the jungle ran rampant, covering everything. Vines and grasses and shoots tangled in every direction, a swath of bright emerald green that felt bright and garish.

Taylor's smile was beatific. Reverent, in silent awe, as he looked around and took one deep breath after another as though he couldn't take in enough of it.

"Wow," he said, when he could speak. "This is beautiful."

Angelica said nothing. She didn't see what left him choked up and emotional. To her it wasn't bad exactly, just not right. There was something that insisted that the place didn't look like a proper jungle. Here the trees grew with twisted roots and hollow trunks, and foxes ran between the boughs and chittered as they turned to look at the visitors.

Here jungle birds sang different songs than in Africa or South America. This was an unfamiliar jungle and would take getting used to.

It felt very far from home.

Angelica screwed a smile on her face as she belatedly realized that her lack of reaction had been duly noted. There was a small crowd of people, all dressed like her, all bearing the unmistakable Viking heritage that Taylor wore: tall and proud, with fair hair and sun-browned skin. One of the milling crowd was the man who had driven them to the compound from the airport. He waved cheerfully when she met his eyes across the clearing.

She squeezed Taylor's arm in a desperate attempt to not be separated and continued on to the swelling number of people gathering under the open pavilion. All of them were dressed the same as they were, clothing easy to slip out of if they shifted.

It was another strange feeling, the sense that she was surrounded by big cats, cautious predators waiting for a misstep, something to prove that she didn't belong there.

The fear and suspicion seemed only to plague her mind. When their host shouted it was with welcome, a gregarious smile and wave accompanying his words. "Welcome, Taylor! Welcome, Angelica! Please, come join us!"

The smiling faces and quizzical looks went a long way to soothe Angelica's upset stomach. They seemed welcoming, even encouraging.

Only the white clothing, the shout and wave, were all too reminiscent of Mr. Roarke on that old TV show she used to watch on cable when she was a kid. The visitors to *Fantasy Island* never fared very well initially, and Mr. Roarke wasn't always quite sincere.

So help me, if anyone shouts, 'de plane de plane' I'm out of here.

"How...how did you know to come get us at the airport?" Taylor asked, and for a moment Angelica was disconcerted, the question coming hard on the heels of her own morbid thoughts. "And please don't say, 'Wait for the elders'—I'm sure they wouldn't mind giving out that much information."

Taylor's question was careful. He was being the agent again, digging for information. Maybe he didn't quite trust the people here either. Angelica moved a little closer to him, somewhat reassured that maybe she wasn't the only one on edge.

But their host shook his head. "Actually, they asked me to give you some updates. For example, all members of your ambush are accounted for, and are safely in Canada."

"Ambush?" Angelica felt her face go pale.

"A pride of lions, a murder of crows, an ambush of tigers," Taylor explained with a soft chuckle. "I'd forgotten you likely hadn't heard that before. Most haven't."

"That's the problem with English," their guide said with a twinkle in his eye. "Even the English don't speak it."

Fine, joke at her expense. At any rate, they knew Taylor's family was safe. She glanced at him, seeing that his jaw had visibly relaxed. He'd been carrying that tension for too long now.

"The entire town got away?" she asked the guide, for the first time realizing that she couldn't remember having heard his name. One more frustrating aspect to this day, to this conversation, to being in a place where once again she didn't know the rules.

Some of that frustration must have shown on her face, because his bushy eyebrows rose in confusion and his head turned to one side as a dog's does when trying to learn a new trick. He glanced at Taylor. "A town of tigers? I'm sorry, I don't know this term."

"I mean..." Angelica explained, hands out, pleading for him to understand her. "Was anyone hurt or... lost?"

He nodded, and she saw for the first time the sadness in the depths of his clear blue eyes. "I'm sorry to say that there was a loss. You father mentioned a Mrs. Petrov. Do you know her?" She could feel the tension in Taylor as he clenched. It would take him time to absorb that news.

"I'm so sorry," she whispered, squeezing Taylor's hand, letting him know she was there for him.

"Your father also told me to tell you that she 'acquitted herself as nobly as her husband had.' I trust that has a significant meaning. But the journey was too much for her at her age. She was *not* taken."

"Thank you, Olaf," Taylor said thickly.

OLAF. You'd think she'd have remembered that name. Now that she looked at him, she could kind of see the shape of the snowman from that kid's movie. Even his nose had a somewhat carrot-like shape that, once seen, could not be unseen. Angelica blinked. This really wasn't the time for that. "How do you know…"

"We are in contact with the colony." Olaf smiled, seeming glad to be able to at least answer that question easily enough. "Through short wave. I listen to a great amount of radio, that's how I learn languages."

Which meant no internet. No way of knowing what the rest of the world was doing. Or whether they were still being pursued. Angelica took a shaky breath. Well, at least they had *some* information, even if it was a little spotty. "You speak English well," she said, and actually meant it. "It's very impressive."

Olaf nodded, pleased at the compliment. "Thank you. I have been given the honor of being your interpreter for the duration of your stay. There is a woman, Leena, who is learning the language, and who will interpret for you if the two of you are ever apart."

Apart? Angelica shot a panicked glance at Taylor, who didn't seem unduly concerned. In fact, he was still back on the trail of figuring out their hosts.

"When can we see the elders?" Taylor asked, eyeing the group that still ranged around them, watching this interchange in a silence that had become eerie.

"Ah!" Olaf held up a finger. "First you eat with the..." he looked to Angelica "...town? And get to know us; that, too, is part of what you seek."

Taylor took a breath to contradict him, Angelica knew he wanted to get on with whatever the point was in being here, whatever process or magical cure that could help her random shifts and difficult way it was forced into her. But as soon as he inhaled, her stomach let out a loud and long lament that brought smiles to the natives, and a flood of color to her cheeks.

"I'm so sorry," she murmured, clutching her belly and feeling the heat on her face.

"Don't be." He smiled. "COME! We will serve our lost... townies?" He said something to the crowd in another language. The crowd let out a cheer and turned as one to lead the way to another part of the compound.

"Thank you." Angelica smiled and, reaching for Taylor's hand, trailed after their host and the horde that led them. *Olaf,* she reminded herself so she wouldn't forget again. *His name is Olaf.*

"We can't let him think 'townie' is correct," Taylor said out of the corner of his mouth.

"Better than 'ambushers,'" Angelica replied, and smiled and waved to the man when he looked back to see why they were lagging so far behind.

Apparently, the group dined together at a series of tables under a roof that looked nowhere near substantial enough to stand up to the rains that were typical in jungle areas. Angelica craned her neck to examine the leafy fronts that seemed to grow over a metal frame, making the space below an actual 'living room.' The area under the roof held a grouping of tables and chairs, with servers, young people that were maybe in their teens and early 20s moving between the tables, setting out platters of food. They took the seats offered and sat, Olaf sitting with them.

"Olaf. It's an unusual name for Nepal, isn't it?" Angelica asked as she settled on her chair. She couldn't get the image out of her head of the singing snowman and needed something else to tie the name to.

Olaf looked at her for a long moment and then laughed. "Oh, I forgot, you are not of the same town as the pilgrims of Taylor's." He turned and spoke in rapid tongue to the woman next to him, who rolled her eyes and clapped him on the back. She turned to Angelica, her eyes merry and bright, and with smile said something she didn't understand. She looked to be the same age as Olaf, with white hair intricately braided into one long plait that traveled down her back nearly to her waist. She laughed as she spoke, using her hands to emphasize words that Angelica didn't understand.

"She says, 'Now you've done it, it's his favorite story,'" Olaf translated good-naturedly.

She responded with another long string of words and he looked back at Angelica. "She says now you won't be able to shut me off." He shook his head a little. "I think that is the right word for it. And she's right."

"I would love to hear it." Angelica looked skeptically at the plate of mush that was set before her by a dark-haired youth who presented the plate with the grand gesture of a maître d' at a five-star restaurant. Somewhat mystified and more than a little wary, she watched Taylor break off a piece of what looked like flat bread and scoop some of the yellow on to it and pop it in his mouth.

"The red stuff is very hot," he said, licking the substance in question off a finger, with the equanimity of one who has been many places and has no problem fitting in wherever he might be.

Olaf broke off a piece of his own bread and used it as a pointer. "Many years ago men from the north traveled all over the globe, exploring and conquering. Sometimes they went home to get their wives and children to live in the lands they took. But many times this was not the case. Some of them were hired by foreign kings as mercs."

She looked at Taylor to clarify. He finished chewing and swallowed the food in his mouth before answering her unspoken question. "Mercenaries. And try the yellow. It's good. Tangy."

Angelica took a cautious bite and her tongue rolled over and begged for more. She loaded up the flatbread and went back to listening to Olaf's tale.

"Mercenaries," Olaf said, with a nod at Taylor for supplying the word. "Some of the most powerful of the mercenaries served the greatest kings of Russia and Ukraine. But some of them, maybe the elders know how, some were cursed or blessed with the shifting. They craved the jungle, the green and the open places to run and hunt. They came here, but did not conquer. They came because they were called evil... Magic... uh, makers. And they were hunted. I am Olaf, named for one of the first that came with wives and weapons and fire."

"You're a long way from the water for a Viking long ship," Angelica mused between mouthfuls. "Why here?"

"Because it was defensible," a strong female voice said.

Angelica looked up into the eyes of a woman whose face reflected many years of hard living, but her eyes held the challenge of youth. Her bearing was straight and slender, her shoulders unbowed, and her smiled revealed bright, white teeth. She came and stood at the empty place opposite Angelica, making no move to sit.

"If you're done with your repast," she said, smiling as she pointed to Angelica's plate.

With a start Angelica realized she'd completely cleaned the plate, including the 'red stuff' that was only now registering the promised burn. She gasped and downed the water in a single gulp. It was the best thing she'd ever had to drink, and she found herself blinking at the empty cup and wondering how to get some more.

"It's from a mountain spring," the old woman said, laughing. "The earth gives to those who will toil." It sounded rote, or perhaps more like a prayer.

"If you are done, the elders would like to interview you. If you would come with me?"

Angelica glanced at Taylor, who shrugged.

Well, I've come all this way... it would be foolish to not talk to them.

Angelica rose, turning to thank Olaf, but the man had his head down, in deference to this woman. Angelica noticed that the entire collection of men and women and children were bowing or even kneeling to her as she passed. She looked at Taylor, whose face mirrored her own confusion. Cautious, and maybe a little protective, he took Angelica's hand and led her around the table in the wake of the woman's strong, straight back.

They left the gathering in an eerie, unnatural silence.

Chapter 16

Angelica's hands were sweating. It was one thing to be on the yellow brick road for several days, but it was another to see the wizard face to face. Taylor felt his own heart beating quickly. There were questions he wanted to ask Olaf, about the township in Minnesota—his father in particular. About the separation, about so many things.

He would've preferred the information before the elders spoke to him, but he was going to have to ask them and try to wing his responses. So far, the impressive woman spoke flawless English. He hoped that would be the case for them all.

They were taken down a long winding pathway that led into a little grotto. The trail they took did not look well-used. Leafy fronds almost hid several of the turns, and had there not been a guide it would have taken some work to not get lost. This was the point, Taylor knew. They took the newcomers on a little-used path, that it might not be easily found again. For all their claims of wanting to help Angelica and Taylor, they were being protective of their own.

Taylor could respect that.

The grotto itself was unexpected. The path angled downhill and ended in what would have been a cave had the top not been open to the sky. Or at least it would have had there not been so many trees along the upper edge that it gave a somewhat leafy roof to the place which allowed for a somewhat filtered light to reach the forest floor. Tall stone walls rose up around them, one end being entirely taken up by a small waterfall that tumbled down from a height of about twelve feet into a pond the size of a small house. Like the rest of the jungle Eden, there truly was more greenery than his eyes could take in comfortably. Even so, his tiger senses adapted to it quickly. Beside him, he heard Angelica gasp.

Two men stood by the little pond, waiting for them. They turned as the group entered. They too wore the white outfits. The heads that lifted to regard them were grey and heavily lined, giving them both the appearance of great age. But they walked as straight as Olaf did, and had sharp eyes. One, at least, appeared to be a bit amused and grinned as the small group entered the grotto between two rocky outcroppings.

"You'll forgive the slight delay." Their guide, the woman with the long silver braid down her back, seemed truly apologetic. She indicated the group with one hand. "As you can see, not everyone is here. We're waiting for the rest of our members."

It was a statement. Taylor had no way of knowing that this wasn't the full group. A test of sorts? Or was she simply being polite?

"Here I was kind of expecting a dark chamber with high chairs and an ominous desk. Maybe something more in keeping with the Illuminati," Angelica whispered.

Taylor stifled a laugh. He hadn't thought of it, but that would be more in keeping with the solemnity of meeting the elders.

"Too uncomfortable," one of the men said, smiling, causing Angelica to twitch. She clearly hadn't expected to be overheard. Taylor watched with narrowed eyes as the man walked over to join them, and wondered what other abilities they held. Despite the wrinkles in his face and the appearance of great age, he moved as briskly and as sure-footedly as a teenager. "At our age, straight-back chairs are a form of punishment." He held his hand out to Taylor. "I'm Sergei." He pointed to the other man. "This is Orlan."

"And I'm Helga," the woman who had escorted them said, and ducked her head a little. "I should have said something before. I'm unused to strangers and don't always remember the little, how you say, courtesies."

"Forgive me," Sergei laughed. "I assumed you introduced yourself before. Tell me, children, you've come a long way to see us. Why?"

"Don't you think it would be better to wait for Alexa?" Helga asked, putting up a hand to stop him.

"Alexa can catch up," Sergei said with a shrug. He turned and shot a few words to the other old man, who laughed and replied in the same tongue.

"She does have her reasons," Helga replied, but without heat.

Taylor took a deep breath but it was Angelica who spoke, cutting right to the chase. "I changed into a shifter. I wasn't born this way. Someone turned me into one."

Sergei's eyebrow lifted and he looked at Helga, who repeated the information for Orlan. He spat out a series of syllables that, even though Taylor didn't know the language, held enough incredulity that the meaning was obvious to all listeners even without the translation.

Angelica's back went straight, her jaw set. She clearly was mad as hell. This was the woman who had fought her way through med school and jungles both to get where she needed to go, and she wasn't used to not being believed. She glanced at Taylor, and added, "And Taylor needs help, too."

It was his turn to be caught by surprise. He grabbed her arm and opened his mouth to stop her. This was none of her business, and especially none of theirs, but she rushed on all the same.

"He shares consciousness with the inner cat. They communicate openly. And he can partially shift, like not all the way, and not all over." She paused to look at him then, and there was a certain sadness in her eyes that told him she didn't like doing what she was doing. But the steel underneath likewise told him she didn't regret doing it. "I'm worried about you."

And here he simply wanted to help his mate. To fix what might not be able to be fixed. So much for keeping a few good cards on hand. Why not throw it all out there before there was a chance to make sure they could trust these strangers? Why not dive in head first? Sink or swim was the option today.

The three faces now looked at him with some speculation.

Taylor's entire body went rigid. She had no right to do this.

"Is this true?" another voice asked, and the group turned to greet the new arrival. Angelica stifled a scream and grabbed Taylor's arm hard enough to hurt. Taylor was beyond feeling it, though, what he saw... He blinked, shook his head to clear it, but the same sight greeted him no matter what he did.

She might have been something out of an artist's imagination, a drawing or an anime. His brain didn't want to accept she was real.

A woman, no doubt at all about the gender, stood unclothed before them. But then she had no use of clothing, as she was covered in a thick, white fur. Her head was almost fully realized as a tiger, but the teeth were still human. Her hands were hands and not paws, but little ivory claw tips protruded from each one. The same held with her feet. Her knees bent back like a human, her pelvic bone was human, but by all appearances she was a two-legged tiger.

"How remarkable for someone so young," she said, coming forward and staring at Taylor speculatively. "I'm Alexa," she said, "and I'm caught up. I'm pleased to meet you." Although her words were directed to both of them, her attention was entirely on Taylor. He shifted uneasily under the scrutiny.

"We have much to discuss," Helga said, and swept an arm to a series of pillows in a large circle around a cheery fire.

"Tiger, tiger, burning bright," Taylor said under his breath, not realizing he'd said it out loud until Helga answered.

"Let's hope it doesn't come to that, shall we?"

More than a little uneasy and definitely still miffed at Angelica, Taylor settled on one of the cushions, thinking it perhaps more suited to the cat than to him. He wanted to ask Alexa about her appearance, but the desire to understand several other points took precedence. Instead, he started with the obvious. "How did my father contact you?"

"We never actually lost touch with our colonists," Helga said, meeting his gaze squarely. "We do rely on short-wave radio, though it has to get bounced a bit. Since the skies were filled with satellites, that's become a lot easier."

"So you knew all along that they were coming for my family?"

"No. We knew your family was safe. That was the first we'd heard about the attack," Alexa corrected, her head tilted to the side, still studying him intently.

Sergei broke off translating for Orlan and added, "You must understand, young Taylor, this is not the first intrusion nor is it the last. Here in the jungles, we have carved a sanctuary. We intended that we be forgotten. The locals think of us as unimportant. They leave us alone because they do not know we are here."

"And in the overall scheme of the world, we're largely useless," Helga said, but the words held a note of bitterness.

"That's not entirely fair, Helga," Sergei corrected her. "With the internet now, we are designers and programmers. Many options have opened to us."

Beside him, Angelica started in surprise.

"But we hide and maintain our ineffectiveness to stay safe. No, Sergei, it is the colonists who enter the world and risk so much to have vitality."

Orlan spat out several words in rapid-fire retort. Sergei looked at the two women and nodded. He addressed Taylor and Angelica both. "I am reminded that it is you two who have set the precedence here today. Our problems will remain, but they are *our* problems. In answer to your question, your father let us know that they were in Canada and settling in well."

"All but one," Taylor mumbled bitterly before he could catch himself.

"Yes, your Mrs. Petrov. She will be remembered with great honor." Helga's look was one of great sadness. "In the meantime, we want to address the two of you. Your father did *not* inform us of your ability, Mr. Mann."

"He didn't know," Angelica interrupted. "It kind of came on him... unexpectedly."

Taylor shot a glance at her.

She met his gaze fiercely, without flinching. "I am *not* risking you. I don't know what that woman did to you, but I can't—"

"Stop, Angelica. Just stop." She'd invaded his privacy. This wasn't her story to tell. Her eyes pleaded with him to understand, but he wasn't ready to just pull her into his arms and forget everything. This whole relationship with the inner cat was too new and fragile still—and here it was, thrown out for the world to see when he was still figuring it out.

His eyes went to Sergei. It was all he could do to speak. "I haven't told anyone but her."

"It's a state that few ever enter," Alexa said, speaking for the others. "In the two hundred years I've been alive, I've never heard of it happening to someone so young. You are indeed a puzzle, young cub."

"What about her?" Taylor asked, pointing at Angelica.

"Do tell us more of what happened, please."

Angelica explained about Africa and Dr. Johns' experiments. As a doctor, she'd been used to giving reports on patients. For the most part she drew on that skill now, giving the basics without emotional delivery, treating the matter clinically until it came down to the moments when she'd changed for the first time. But it was the things done to him that made her voice waver and break.

She dashed away tears with the back of her hand. Taylor reached for her then, placing a hand on her leg, letting her know he was still there, despite his own anger.

"She has no inner cat," Taylor said, drawing the attention from her to himself, that she might compose herself.

"This Dr. Johns. Very evil creature," Sergei said, brows furrowed thoughtfully. "You say she was funded by..."

"An even more evil woman. The head of a drug cartel," Angelica all but spat the words. This, too, was still a rather raw experience for her. "She saw Taylor shift."

"Regrettable," Helga murmured, "but not unique. Such things have happened before. But to address your statement, things are not as you think. All men and women have an inner beast. It lives in us, feeds from us, and we nourish it. The animal needs not be personified as rage or hate. It can be as fine as a housecat, or as friendly as a dog."

"Bite your tongue," Alexa said with a smile.

"She just has to find it. Wouldn't you say?" Sergei said with an eyebrow raised in Helga's direction.

"Agreed."

The four elders stood in mute contemplation. Too silent. Too still for a long moment. Taylor began to wonder about the stories he'd heard of the elders holding great magick. Were they communing somehow in the silence? Speaking in a non-verbal way that he couldn't comprehend?

Maybe they just can't figure us out. There's a great big jungle to run in. Get the mate and let's go.

It was a tempting thought. Taylor was ready to do just that.

"I will take the male," Alexa said, breaking the silence.

Take the male?

"Agreed. And I the female," said Helga. She rose gracefully and spoke only to Angelica. "Come, child," she said, and once more turned her back and walked off, expecting to be obeyed.

Angelica shot Taylor a glance, but surprisingly she obeyed.

I don't like this one bit.

Chapter 17

By the time Angelica made it back to the room, she was nearly dead from exhaustion. It was an almost anticlimactic day, but somehow the whole thing left her drained and irritable. First Helga had sat her down and interviewed her. They spoke of everything under the sun, right down to grade school drama and high school crushes. She'd found out about all those long nights spent working while in residency. About the insufferable jackass who taught anatomy, and the even more insufferable jackass who taught calculus. When Helga found out that Angelica had taken a great many classes in Latin suddenly Orlan was able to communicate with her, though some of the Latin left her stumped. It had been a long time, and she was rusty with the concept of speaking it. Still, they'd managed to communicate fairly well, all things considered.

But she never forgot this was an interrogation as much as an interview.

Angelica had been forced to say the same things over and over, rephrasing things, rehashing key points. She was pushed, verbally if not physically. It didn't seem to matter how many different ways she'd already said something, they'd ask again. Looking for lies, she realized. Traps. They didn't trust her. Maybe she couldn't blame them for that. Their entire existence was predicated on the idea of their society being kept secret. She likely wasn't the first to try to infiltrate this inner circle. Somehow, she only needed to make them understand that she was there for help.

Even if she was getting peeved all the same.

Look, they can't help me if they don't understand what's going on. And to do that they have to understand who I am. And even more that I'm worthy of that help.

But even knowing that didn't make things any easier. She had to physically remind herself often that the old woman was trying to help. And if they didn't know what to do with her, they at least had the best educated guess on the planet.

So she found herself with her temper flared most of the day. She needed something she could latch on to as she admonished herself to stay calm. The only thing she had anymore was Taylor, and he'd been none too pleased with her when they'd parted. Maybe she'd been a little eager to get away, recognizing the anger in every line of his body that had flared the moment she'd opened her big mouth.

But she'd needed to. He required help right now every bit as much as she did. It killed her inside to think that he had been altered, too. He never should have even been in Africa. It had been she who'd brought him there, who'd changed everything, all for the sake of a little girl that no one had even been able to find once the whole mess was over.

All of this is my fault. And yet, somehow, I think I have the right to cling to Taylor, to focus on him now, to cling to him when everything gets overwhelming? Maybe I need to learn to stand on my own two feet.

And so the mantra of, 'Taylor is here. Taylor is with me' gradually morphed into something more along the lines of, 'I can do this. I'm strong. I'm capable. These people don't scare me.'

Which worked for a while. At least up until Helga brought out the exercises Angelica had been suffering through for the last month, culminating with that trip to Minnesota.

It was too much. In that moment she snapped and informed Helga exactly what she could do with her exercises. Of course, Angelica apologized right away and she was very sorry for losing her temper like that. After all, Helga didn't deserve it. But the damage was done and Helga seemed withdrawn after that, becoming cold and distant.

Angelica spent the next hour trying to be all happiness and contrition, but Helga seemed more aloof with each passing moment. When the old woman finally called an end to their day, Angelica trudged back to their assigned room with a heavy burden on her shoulders—one she could only bear by thinking of the one who was likely already waiting for her.

Thank goodness for Taylor.

But the room was empty. She'd hoped he would be there, hoped he could soothe her wounds and salvage the rest of the day. Instead, she fell into bed alone and stared at the ceiling fan as it made its maddeningly slow rotations.

She must have napped because the slamming door shattered her nerves and shook her awake. Taylor stood in the doorway, seething and growling from deep within his chest.

"What happened to you?" she asked, sitting up in bed, shoving her hair back from her face and blinking sleepily at him.

"I'll tell you what happened," Taylor growled, his face a mask of dark clouds as his fingers clenched and unclenched. "Turn your right hand, NO! The other right. Just one claw, not two! I probably would have changed all four of them at once and then where would we be? The whole damn world depends on if I can keep *them* happy."

Angelica sighed. He'd had a bad day, too. Here she'd wanted to curl up in his arms, to feel again that incredible intimacy they'd shared after the bath, but he was too worked up for that.

"What now?" He looked at her sharply. He must have heard the sigh and identified it for what it was. Frustration. Irritation.

"Nothing..." Angelica rearranged herself against the pillows, sitting cross-legged as she watched Taylor pace around the room. She hated this. Hated the tension that came between them so easily ever since she'd become a lion. It was the same tension she'd felt ever since they'd returned to the States from Africa. Here it was again, the same distance she thought they had finally bridged, all the resentment that they'd tried so hard to deny, to suppress.

He stopped suddenly, and threw up his hands. "Why the hell did you tell them about me? We came here for your problem. I don't have a problem."

She didn't know what to say initially. She met his gaze squarely, not cringing, not running away. *He's not his father. Look at him, so angry, so frustrated, and trying so hard to keep it under control. You know he's not going to hurt you, so why is it so damn hard to speak?*

It was because she wanted to choose her words carefully. Each one mattered so much right now. "You're sharing headspace with a large predator, but you don't see that as an issue?"

Whoops. That hadn't come out quite as well as it had sounded in her head.

"Not compared to... to Tigra! Or whatever she is, half-human, half-tiger. Do you know why she stays halfway like that? This is a keeper. It's because she has arthritis. She *still* has arthritis in the cat form but the human and the cat have it in different places, so if she's half and half, she cuts down the pain. She's in mid-shift because she can't take a damn Tylenol!"

He pushed past her and stalked to the bathroom. The door banged behind him, hard enough to make her jump. A second later she heard the water run. Angelica sat on the edge of the bed and stared at the dresser, trying to calm herself. But, truth be told, she was pretty mad herself right now. She'd only been trying to help. She'd only *ever* been trying to help.

Taylor walked out of the bathroom, drying his face with a towel. She got to her feet, feeling disadvantaged in sitting down. She needed him to hear what she had to say.

He stopped in front of her, arms crossed. Not in the most receptive of moods.

"I'm sorry I mentioned your issue with the voice in your head. I hadn't seen Alexa then and I was worried, especially when I saw your face at the airport. You remember, I'm a doctor. Faces are not supposed to do that, and I was afraid for you. You've been different since Africa. But I've made things worse for you. I'm sorry."

"It's not you," he said, tossing the towel to the floor in frustration. "It's those damn exercises! I don't know what I have to prove; it's not like we're losing our personalities, we're just getting closer together. Why is that such a bad thing?"

Angelica didn't look at him. "Because then *you'll* have no inner cat?" she asked. "Then you'll have to do your exercises to try and find him again." She chuckled, but the sound rang hollow. "But at least you will have had one." The last word came out on what suspiciously sounded like a sob. She cleared her throat, pulled herself together. "Taylor." She placed a hand on his arm, curling her fingers around his bicep. He was so large and muscular and powerful. She loved that arm. Loved him. More deeply than she'd even realized before today. "I'm sorry I spoke out of turn. Your development is your issue and none of mine. I shouldn't mess around in your life and I'm sorry." She rose and kissed his forehead. Taylor's brow was still furrowed, and he was still breathing hard. His eyes were wary.

Distrustful.

And that was what finally did it. If he didn't trust her, what was the point in staying?

So Angelica turned, and calm as she could manage, despite the fact that her hands were shaking, she turned and walked out of the building.

And Taylor, that bastard, let her go.

IT WAS LATE AFTERNOON. The communal meal would be served soon enough, but Angelica didn't exactly feel hungry. What a freakin' waste of time! Why had they thought coming here was going to fix anything? There was too much stress, too much anger, too much change, and now she and Taylor were at each other's throats instead of working together. It wasn't just him starting the fights. She was equally guilty of being on a hair trigger. And right now, she needed him more than ever. She suspected that he needed her, too. And the way things were going, they both needed a babysitter to make them shut up and play nice.

Despite all that, she needed the time alone. A walk seemed like a good idea, especially as it would give her a chance to not only get the lay of the land, but maybe gain a little better understanding of this new world she'd found herself in. Angelica took to the trail that ran through the camp and beyond with something that wasn't exactly eagerness, but was an interest and curiosity that took her outside of herself for a while and allowed her room to think about other things.

The compound sat in the embrace of a mountainside where the jungle crept on its never-ending quest to spread as far as the rains would let it. The leafy world she wandered into was life burgeoning with more life, plants that slowly overtook the impatient animals and men, and ran past them both over the rocks that littered the hillside.

At the end of the drive, a small set of ruts cut through the verge by the tires of infrequent cars and trucks. Here she found a rusted gate with a new chain barring the entrance. It was meant to give the impression that there was nothing along the rutted road worth the effort of trespassing, nothing but old jungle and a long-forgotten sanctuary left to rot in the sultry heat.

The chain was a shining contrast, the padlock one of the best money could buy. She looked at the back of the old, rusted, useless gate and wondered if it ever actually fooled anyone. Behind the time-worn metal and the cheap paint that might once have been a shade of green, bright shining steel beams reinforced the gate with an unbendable will. The dilapidated barbed wire fence that led away from the gate was concealing a high-voltage wire, and there were security cameras nestled in among the trees, one actually in a constructed nest that looked so real that for a moment she thought it was.

Indeed, this group was very skilled at hiding.

She gingerly tested the gate. It wasn't wired. The voltage, apparently, did not include the rusted metal. She stood at the end of the drive, watching the sky begin to bleed—first red, then orange as the sky exploded with deep vibrant colors, the sun giving a final good night to the earth.

She turned back toward the compound, not quite ready to go back, and leaned on the gate, watching the sunset, breathing in the noises and stories of the jungle. As she had been able to smell cancer in the waitress, so could she now smell the stories of the little ones that roamed this jungle. A rabbit crouched nearby, hoping for her to leave so he could finish eating. A fox scurried off, frustrated that she stood there so close to the rabbit, depriving the vixen of her dinner. Birds sang sleepily in the heavy trees. And the man behind her stank of whiskey.

Wait...

She pushed off the gate as hard as she could, panic already trapping the scream within her throat. But he had a hold of the back of her shirt. She thrashed at him, finding her voice as the fabric parted, the easy opening designed for quick removal in shifting, leaving her skin exposed and bare in the twilight shadows. She stumbled into the road, hands coming up to cover herself, and dared a glance back.

He was a local, or at least had the look of a Nepalese, not one of Taylor's misplaced Vikings. He grinned and started to climb the gate. Angelica ran.

She was moving even before she realized she was in motion. There was no way she could outrun him. Her shoes weren't suited to the jungle, and she'd never been particularly fast to begin with. But she had enough time to shift if she could only find a place...

She turned off the road and dove into the underbrush, running down the side of a hill into a trough cut through the ground by a small stream, and there found a thick grouping of trees that would shield her from view.

She shucked off the pants and bent over, thinking, *Be a cat. Think like a cat. Move like a cat. Become the cat.*

"I see you," the man called from nearby in very broken English. "I know you are there. I can smell the fear. Do you know you're mine?"

The intruder—no—the predator circled around the trees, looking for an opening. He reached into his pocket and produced a knife that was more machete than pocketknife. Finding his opening, he thrust the blade blindly into the greenery. Angelica only just barely dodged one such thrust and rolled in desperation, to throw herself further back in among the ferns, praying for invisibility, or at the very least to find the cat that was so far eluding her.

Be a cat. Be a fucking cat.

Withdrawing the blade, her assailant took a step back. Was he searching for movement? Or perhaps just traces of her blood.

If it's blood he wants...

The lioness roared. The would-be predator cried out as the lioness leaped on top of him, knocking the knife from his hands and sending him over backward into the stream behind him. The lioness's full weight came down on his belly, claws raking his skin and forcing the air from his lungs in a giant WHOOSH.

Sanity returned.

I won't kill again.

The lioness twisted and ran, leaving him there. Leaving him to hopefully drown on his own, leaving her own conscience clear of his death. She bolted for the road, stretching out and streaking for the compound as fast as her legs could carry her.

The panic was short-lived. It was one thing to be told there was a lion in Nepal, another to see one running full speed toward the community. Parents gathered children in close, sharp exclamations of surprise greeting her. Suspicion.

Thankfully someone had the forethought to grab a tablecloth and wrap the lioness who collapsed in the communal space where they'd been gathering to dine. She clutched the fabric around herself as best she could and, taking a deep breath, began the transformation back.

"There was someone there! I don't know if he wanted me dead... or for something else..." she gasped when she had enough of her own vocal cords to speak. Careful to not use the more alarming words of 'rape' or 'kidnapping' out of respect for the children who still clung terrified to their parents at the edges of the crowd. Her meaning was clear enough anyway that several started to cry. She hated this. Hating frightening them like this but had to choke out the rest, let them find the man and deal with him. "He was at the gate... and a freakin' big knife."

When she was a child, a cousin set a group of plastic soldiers on a cookie sheet and put them in the oven just to watch them melt. Angelica was seeing that again, here. As one, nearly a dozen men and women suddenly melted, their tear-way clothing doing just that, and within a heartbeat ten tigers were nearly airborne, running down the road in pursuit.

She almost felt sorry for the man.

Almost.

She felt arms wrap around her. The next thing she knew she was in Taylor's strong arms and being carried back to their room. He treated her like spun glass, all concern and solicitation. He checked her for wounds, found a fresh change of clothing in the drawer and helped her dress, leaving the tablecloth crumpled in a heap on the floor.

It was only a few minutes before there was a knock on the door. She was curled up in his arms again, lying on the bed, and didn't want to leave. He tucked the blankets around her until she was in a safe little warm cocoon, letting her stay and not deal with this.

Angelica lay there, accepting the gesture for what it was, though a large part of her was still angry enough to want to go back, to be one of the big cats tearing through the jungle to look for this intruder. To do him the harm she hadn't been able to stomach earlier. Seeing the children frightened had brought home to her how precarious this group's existence could quite possibly be, despite having been settled here for hundreds of years. Who was to say that this group was any safer than the one in Minnesota? Or any other group, however many more there were.

She was such an idiot! Why had she even figured it was okay to leave the compound? She didn't know anything, and to do it after dark? Stupid! Stupid! Stupid!! For a doctor, an intelligent woman, she was a freakin' idiot! She needed to be put on a leash!

She stewed in these thoughts, deep within her blanket nest as Taylor opened the door a crack and talked to someone outside. There was a rumble of voices, a back and forth that she couldn't quite make out before the door opened wide to admit the elder woman, Helga, who came inside and paused in the middle of the room. She held something in her hand that Angelica couldn't see.

Angelica sat up, letting the blanket fall. She caught a glimpse of other people milling around outside on the step before he shut the door gently, closing out the world and the growing outrage that she could feel vibrating through their conversations even from here. For once she was thankful that Taylor had decided things for her, knowing that he had kept the others out, that he would only allow one person inside the room to tend her, and that apparently Helga was the chosen one. It was an audacious move, one that challenged the elders for her sake.

It didn't escape her notice that he'd actually won that point.

Helga moved to lean over her, gentle fingers lifting her chin that she might look Angelica in the eyes. "Are you hurt?"

"No," Angelica said, and realized that she was shaking. "No, just wasn't expecting that. I got caught very off-guard."

"I'm sorry I wasn't with you," Taylor said, sitting next to her, taking her hand in his. Letting Helga know that he would only allow so much interaction, that he would shut things down in an instant if he felt it necessary.

Not that Helga was exactly one to back down either. Her eyes were filled with a certain fire as she turned her gaze on him. "Yes, well, neither of you are going to be going much of anywhere unescorted any time soon." The words were ominous, made more so when she unfolded the paper she was holding in her hand. "We found this on your attacker." She presented it first to Taylor. His face froze in anger. Angelica had seen that expression before. Several people had died the last time she'd seen that look.

Taylor was spoiling for a fight.

She reached out and took the paper from him.

The words weren't legible, but the picture of her and the picture of Taylor were unmistakable. They were also taken while they had been incarcerated in Dr. John's laboratory. Pictures taken during the experiments.

Pictures that weren't supposed to exist.

Angelica swallowed hard, her hand convulsing on the paper, wadding it into a ball in her fist. "What does it say?"

"You have a price on your heads." Helga spat the words. "50 million Rupees for each of you, if alive. Or 20 million if you are... still warm."

"What's that in U.S. money?" Angelica needed a reference. It sounded like a lot, but how much was "a lot?"

Helga looked to Taylor, lost.

"About a half million," Taylor said, taking the paper from her and smoothing it out on the bed between them. "Nepalese Rupees run about 100 per U.S. dollar."

"Enough for a killer or kidnapper to retire and live like a king." Helga's body shook with fury.

"Who would...?"

Taylor pointed to the sole word on the page that she should have noticed herself. That she might have recognized if she'd been looking for it.

"GRISELDA?"

Taylor nodded. "And now they know we're here." He looked at Helga. "Or do they?"

"Someone does. They will return." She grinned suddenly, a very dark and feral grin. "Although that particular man will never tell a soul."

Taylor nodded.

Angelica felt ill.

"There is a very small amount of drug use in Nepal," Helga said after a moment, her voice softening a little. "Mostly, the locals cannot afford it; it's limited to the wealthy." She looked out the window to distant fields. "But poppies grow easily here, as do other sources of drugs. There are organizations like this..." she waved at the paper, "everywhere in the world. They have eyes everywhere. I am afraid you were followed here."

"From the U.S.?" Angelica tried to reason that out. They'd been so careful.

"From Africa I would guess," Taylor said. "It's obvious she had someone there. These pictures..." He rapped the paper with his knuckle. "Griselda will not quit. Ever."

"So what do we do?" Angelica looked between the two of them.

Taylor and Helga were unusually quiet.

Hiding under the blankets again was starting to sound better and better.

Chapter 18

By the time Helga left, Angelica was asleep. He didn't blame her, the day catching up with her all in a rush. That was the problem with adrenaline—the aftermath left you weak as, well, a kitten.

At least Taylor was able to let her get some sleep. So far he'd managed to push away inquiries from concerned individuals. No way in hell was he going to allow an inquisition though, truth be told, he still had plenty of questions himself. Not all of them directed at her.

First was how they'd been found in the first place. The drive in had been long and winding, down paths that were barely rutted sometimes. Someone had to know precisely where the compound was. And from what he'd been able to see thus far, this was a place even the natives in Nepal avoided.

Though, in a very confusing way, wasn't this group considered natives now? Having been here nearly a thousand years?

Thoughts like that made his brain hurt. And what talks that needed to come would have to be saved for later. Right now he had more biological needs to deal with, namely the pursuit of food. It had been too long since they'd eaten, and after the trials of the day a hot meal would go a long way toward restoring their energy, and would better give them the means to deal with whatever was coming next. Because this obviously wasn't over. Not by a longshot.

Taylor ventured out, only to find the mealtime was ending, the leftovers in the process of being packaged and stored for later. He asked for two bowls of the stew, which they gave him, even if the action was a bit begrudging. On the way out of the kitchen he snagged a loaf of bread, and took the entire meal back with him to the room, juggling utensils and bowls awkwardly and wishing he'd thought to ask about a tray.

The community was unusually quiet as he passed through the common areas. Maybe somber was a better word. They'd been in place for near a thousand years; would they have to run now, like his family had to? For the same reason—because he'd brought the evil to them?

Yet he saw no resentment. If there was blame then they were either waiting to share it in discussion, which would likely come in the morning, or they truly faced life with more equanimity than he'd given them credit for. A couple of the women came after him, asking how Angelica was with eyes that were gentle, that reflected genuine concern. He answered that all was well, though in his heart he was unsure. She'd said little, and their communication lately had been lacking. Had he truly known how she'd felt since they left Minnesota? Or, for that matter, Africa? Lately he'd had the suspicion that he couldn't do anything right, triggering a response that had left both him and his cat on edge.

She's frustrated. Scared and frustrated.

But the rest? The basics he knew. It was the finer details, the nuances, that he missed. When had she closed herself off so thoroughly to him?

He slipped into the room, letting the smell of the stew work its magic on her, rousing her from her dreams. She blinked in the dim light from the bathroom, the door being ajar. He reached past her to turn on the lamp on her bedside table, the bulb casting a dim glow that made her face seem shadowed and remote.

"That smells heavenly." Her whisper was deep, throaty. Nearly a purr. He set the bowl on her lap and took a spoonful and brought it to her lips. "I'm able to feed myself," Angelica protested, laughing, but opened her mouth anyway and accepted the spoon. She closed her eyes as she chewed, her expression becoming beatific. "Oh, that is sublime. I definitely need more of that."

Taylor loaded up another spoonful, but she wrapped her hand around his. "Eat yours before it gets cold. I can feed myself."

Taylor nodded, mute and a little miffed that she'd shoved aside his attempt at tender romance, or at least of tender caregiving that might have been a prelude to romance, and retreated to the other side of the bed, sitting with his back against the wall. If he tore the bread in half with a touch more violence than was absolutely necessary to get the job done, well, who was he to say? He handed her half and concentrated on his own dinner, only now realizing how hungry he was.

"I didn't get hurt; you know that, right?"

"I know." He nodded, his voice quiet and terse. "I also know that you were out there alone because of me, because I was so pissed off." He glanced over to her, wondering how to reach her. "You and I have been having issues," he said after a moment. "Tempers, expectations..."

"We're being hunted," Angelica temporized, waving a chunk of bread in the air as though swatting away his words. "By two factions no less, and one of those our own government! I think a little stress is a healthy reaction under the circumstances."

He set down the stew on his side table and put his hand on her leg, a gesture that had become familiar. Comforting. At least he hoped it was. "Be that as it may," he murmured, bending toward her, inviting her to lean on his shoulder. "But if we're being hunted, then we can't be fighting. I suddenly realized I could have lost you today. I don't want to lose you."

She sighed a little and bit her lip. "I've been there. I never want to lose you." She carefully set the spoon down and wriggled until she had her head settled against his. "I happen to love you."

He shifted a little, moving his head so that she had to move hers, until their lips were millimeters apart. Her breath was warm on his cheek. "I love you, too." He kissed her, once, tenderly, lips lingering in the briefest of touches. "And I won't let them hurt you, no matter what they—"

But his words were cut off by a knock on the door. Cursing the timing he turned his head to call out, feeling her draw away, settling again against her own pillow, putting space between them once again. Funny how she'd shifted all of three inches and felt a mile away.

He bit back a curse as Olaf hesitantly opened the door.

"He's one of the ones that shifted," Angelica murmured, and Taylor nodded. Then he owed Olaf thanks, for going after the unknown assailant, for being a part of the group that had kept her, kept all of them from danger.

What's more, Olaf was smiling. He apparently had good news. His grin went from ear to ear and it was almost impossible to not join in.

"I'm sorry to interrupt, but you'll want to hear this. I was on the wireless and getting news from the BBC and I found out that a General Willette has been permanently relieved of duty. It appears the general had a bit of a breakdown. Apparently, it was leaked that he was mobilizing against a town of shape-shifters." Olaf laughed, the sound ringing with the deep satisfaction of seeing someone get their just desserts. "He's in a mental hospital right now, under evaluation."

Taylor smirked. "That sounds like Dad's lawyers at work."

"Wait, it gets better," Olaf said, holding up a hand to forestall comments. "This came out *after* evidence showed up linking him with a child trafficking ring out of Africa. Though, in a rather unofficial statement today, he maintained that they weren't human to begin with, so it wasn't illegal. His own lawyers shut him down pretty fast, but screenshots of various tweets make his position pretty clear, and have gone absolutely viral."

"He's going to be away for a long time. It looks like justice has been served." Angelica laughed, and for the first time in ages he saw the relief in her eyes. She didn't look quite so haunted.

Now if only Griselda could be dealt with as easily.

Olaf waved his hands to get their attention. "There's more! Your government is giving a great deal of money in recompense to your town for their unlawful invasion. And a formal apology has been issued on behalf of the U.S. government."

Taylor blinked. "Really?" His father's lawyers were better than he'd thought.

Olaf nodded, pleased at their stunned reactions. "Apparently, that woman who was killed in the invasion—"

"Mrs. Petrov."

"Petrov, yes. Well, her heirs have filed a wrongful dead complaint."

"Wrongful death," Angelica corrected automatically.

Taylor blinked. "Wait, what heirs? She had no children."

"The town is acting as heirs," Olaf said. "So your tiger town is going to be even richer."

Taylor shook his head. Money could never replace that life. Or the feeling of safety that had been ripped from them. Taylor's family would never return to Minnesota. Though he supposed that the cash would go a long way toward setting up a new community elsewhere.

It would take a long time before they felt secure, though.

I did that. I took that from them.

As though sensing where his thoughts were going, Angelica reached over and grabbed his arm. "Listen to me. Or to Olaf. You know what this means, right? Nothing is your fault. This was all on that general. Not you. It was his obsession that led to this. You did nothing wrong."

Olaf looked uncertainly from one to the other. "I should probably go. I'm only the messenger and it seems you have things to... discuss. I will likely be talking to your town tonight over the shortwave. I'll come and get you at the appointed time, but it will likely be in the middle of the night."

It was his fault that things had become so awkward. Taylor rose and went to clasp the man's arm gratefully. "You bring good news. Thank you, Olaf."

Olaf gave a terse nod and disappeared out the door, closing it behind him so softly that it barely made a sound. Taylor realized then just how gracefully the other man moved, and wondered if perhaps he too had a closer relationship to his own cat than Taylor had realized.

"I didn't realize how much all of this was weighing on me," Angelica said as the door closed behind Olaf. She shook her head and stared at the now-cold bowl of stew still in her hands.

Taylor opened his mouth to speak and found that he couldn't. His mouth opened and closed a couple of times, and finally he just shrugged and fell into more than sat in the chair nearest the door. Suddenly he was very tired. This whole day, the arguments, the news, the blame that had been on his shoulders had left him crumbled... no, shattered inside. He dropped his head into his hands. Even if Angelica was right, and the blame wasn't his to carry, the outcome still was. His family would never be the same. A great woman had lost her life.

He couldn't shake the feeling that he should have prevented it somehow.

His shoulders shook in silent sobs, the anguish so great that he could no longer hold it back. Eventually he became aware of Angelica kneeling on the floor next to him, her head pressed against his arm as she tried to peer up at him in concern. Her own eyes brimmed with unshed tears, not crying for the reasons that he was, but instead crying *because* he was. This, too, was overwhelming, but in a different way that brought a sweet ache to his heart. He brushed his hand across his eyes, wiping away the tears, trying to smile for her sake.

"Thank you."

"Are you okay?" Her head tilted to the side as she considered him.

He touched her furrowed brow, trying to smooth the lines away with his thumb. "Yeah." He swallowed hard to get past the lump in his throat. "Yeah. I just..."

Angelica spread his knees apart and sidled in between them, so that she could rest her head on his thigh. His breath caught in his throat as he reached to tangle his fingers in her hair. At least he tried to. It was his claws that got tangled, dark strands winding chaotically around his paw.

ANGELICA DIDN'T NOTICE anything strange at first. She stroked his leg and told him that she loved him and that it was all going to work out. She felt his hand on her head, in her hair. It felt... odd, heavy, warm. She opened her eyes and found Taylor looking like the Elder, halfway between, still man in bone and sinew, but covered in tiger fur and one hand at least transformed into a full tiger paw. That was the one on her head, in her hair.

"The cat wanted to touch you," Taylor said with an apologetic shrug. He drew his hand back, embarrassed. Fur began to recede along his arm.

"I'm his mate, too," she said softly, reaching for his arm, drawing him back, smiling and leaning into his caress.

Taylor's eyes lost focus for a moment and then smiled. "He wants to know..." He hesitated. "He wants to know if your cat would curl up and sleep with him. I told him that you need to resist the temptation to do that until the elders can be sure you won't stay that way. Changing today—that was dangerous."

"It was more dangerous to get captured," she reminded him, shuddering a little.

"Yeah," he said quietly. "I don't... I can't lose you."

Angelica reached up to stroke the thick fur on his cheek. "But I'm his mate, too. Taylor, I can't change, I don't dare, but I would be pleased to snuggle in bed with a tiger. A literal one. It might be kind of cozy."

Taylor smiled and finished the shift as he climbed into bed. Angelica noticed that the transformation no longer seemed to be causing him pain.

Interesting.

With a start, she realized something else. The voice in her head that memorized all her medical knowledge was silent. For the first time since medical school it didn't catalogue every illness, every physical malady. For that matter, it had been silent for a while now. It hadn't even spoken when she smelled the cancer on the waitress back in Minnesota.

"Tay..." She turned, but the tiger was lying across the bed, licking his lips. There was no point in attempting conversation. Besides, it wasn't all that important. They could talk in the morning.

And the tiger did look awfully content. And like he was going to take up more than his fair share of the bed.

It's kind of like sleeping with a house cat. A very big house cat.

Still a little dubious, she lifted his front paw. The cat stayed in place. Angelica slipped under the giant paw and rested her head against the strong shoulder. She'd left her clothing on so the fur wouldn't tickle quite so much, and because the idea of sleeping naked with a big furry animal just felt weird. But the tiger, that is, Taylor, wrapped his great paw gently around her, cocooning her in his arm, safe and secure. And she found that sleeping curled up to warm fuzzy animal felt very cozy indeed.

ANGELICA WOKE JUST before the knock sounded on the door. She must have heard the footsteps on the front step. Taylor, naked and definitely very much a man, was sleeping pressed behind her, one arm thrown casually over her, his head buried in her hair.

"Taylor." She rose on one arm, senses on the alert. For a moment she panicked, expecting the worst, still rattled from the intruder of the day before.

Wait. They said they'd wake you, remember?

Taylor woke when the knock sounded. "What?" He sat up, groggy and disoriented, rubbing one hand over his face. "What time is it?"

"No idea," Angelica said, rising and grabbing at his clothing that he'd left discarded on the floor when he'd transformed. She handed it to him. "I assume they're talking to your father. They said they'd come."

Taylor was up and dressed before he was even awake, or so she guessed. He was at the door in less time than it took to think about it and pulled it open. He said something to someone outside that she couldn't quite make out and then turned back to her. "I said we'd be there in a minute." His eyes went to the bed, the blankets that were strewn across the floor. "Didn't I..." He pointed at the mess with a frown. "Wasn't I in cat form..."

Angelica kicked a blanket aside, looking for her shoes. She glanced up and shrugged. "He must have changed back. I'm surprised I never noticed. I must've been exhausted."

"*He* changed..." His eyes lost focus again and he nodded. "It seems so. And you didn't shift? Do you remember? I don't. I... Are you coming?"

It seemed he was spending an awful lot of time on inner dialogue lately. She squelched the momentary jealousy that came from being left out and sat up in triumph, holding up her missing shoe. "You really don't mind?"

"Of course not." He turned and waved her to follow. Hopping on one foot as she slipped the other on, she followed.

They trailed Olaf under a bright moon, the pathways treacherous under the deep shadows. Olaf and Taylor seemed to be adept at finding solid ground, but Angelica stumbled more than once and cursed the fact that she couldn't get her cat self to cooperate with night vision that way that Taylor could with his cat. More and more she was growing disgusted at her own hodgepodge of abilities, and hoped they'd come up with some kind of answer for her.

He led them down a path Angelica was fairly sure she'd never seen in daylight, ending at a small building tucked deep under the trees. Here was another room identical in shape to theirs. But that's where the similarities ended. It's what it held that made it very, very different.

The room was covered in tile: floor, ceiling, and walls. It was like being in a giant shower stall, making the space downright chilly. There were two seats, both of them tall stools, but the bulk of the room was taken by the very last thing she expected to see in the wilds of Nepal.

A rack of servers was humming in the corner. Patch cables strung from one to another and ran up into a pipe in the ceiling. Another rack held a half-dozen routers. And that was just the stuff she could identify. Then there were the other items that were plugged in and lit up that looked vaguely computerish that Angelica couldn't begin to guess at.

Honestly, if she hadn't briefly dated a computer geek in college she'd never have known that the boxy things in the corner were servers. The whole room was well beyond her expertise.

But it was a long way from being a short-wave radio. Nor did it mesh with the whole lack of technology that she'd been led to believe was part of life in the jungle.

She turned in a slow circle, trying to take it all in. The room had a stash of laptops, some in pieces all over the work table, most parked in a safe slot big enough to store them. These were numbered and, though she couldn't read the writing, the sign-out sheet was a universal constant. It was likely that if aliens from another planet came to visit, they would have a sign-out sheet for equipment that looked exactly the same somewhere on the mothership.

"You have an IT center?" Taylor asked, following the lines of wires with his eyes.

Olaf looked at him in surprise. "Of course. Most of us work on the internet now. It pays the bills."

"But how?"

"Please. I'll be happy to answer all questions, but there is a limited time to talk to those of your town. You must hurry or lose the curtain."

"Window," Angelica corrected automatically, shrinking away from Olaf as he came near to flip a switch on a piece of equipment behind her.

"You will lose that, too," he said, motioning frantically to a radio setup she hadn't even seen until now. It was the lowest-tech thing in the room, and even that looked fairly new and expensive. If she had to guess, she'd think it was in all likelihood a piece of equipment that, like the rest, was top of the line.

Olaf hurried them to the bench and flipped a second switch on a large radio. "The antenna is on the top of the mountain," he explained. "Laying the cable was a... bee-yotch." He looked at them and smiled at his use of the word. "Did I say that right?"

Angelica nodded. It gave her something to do to keep from laughing hysterically. She was starting to feel a little like Alice. All that was lacking was the white rabbit. It occurred to her that this was the second time recently that she'd pulled out an Alice in Wonderland metaphor and wondered if this was her life now, something just this surreal.

"Here." He shoved a microphone at Taylor, along with a pair of headphones. Taylor put one side of the headphones against his ear and leaned into the mic. "Hello?" Angelica saw his expression soften. "Hey, Mom. Yeah, I can't hear you too well... what? No, she's okay" He motioned for Angelica to sit next to him and take the other side of the headphones. She sat and held the other side up to her ear, feeling a little like she was intruding.

...Good, have they been able to help her yet?"

"We're working on it," Angelica said into the mic, realizing that the conversation was about her.

"Oh, Angelica? Is that you, dear?"

"Yeah, Mom," Taylor said, answering for her. "We're both here."

"Good! Angelica, sweetie. I'm so glad you're there where it's safe."

"We heard that..." Taylor hesitated, his hand covering his mouth. His glistened, and he seemed to be struggling what to say.

Mrs. Petrov...

"—that everyone is all right now," Angelica finished, knowing they didn't have time to get into it. She reached for his hand, squeezing it. Taylor nodded his thanks to her,

"Yes, we're fine now. Our legal team came through and a lot of that was due to your father."

"Dad?" Taylor said, holding the speaker close to his ear. "I was expecting him to be on the radio. Where is he?"

"He's gone, dear!" His mother's voice was fading fast, being replaced by a beeping that almost sounded like Morse code. Angelica glanced up to Olaf, startled, motioning that they were having trouble. Olaf seemed unsurprised, standing behind them, arms crossed, face implacable.

"Gone? Where?"

"He left yest—" And suddenly his mother was gone.

Only the signal was left on the radio.

Taylor looked up at Olaf, "Can you get her back?" he asked, his voice thick with emotion.

Olaf looked at his watch and shook his head. "Sorry, on Mondays the signal is very short. It gets overridden by someone in the South China Sea. I don't actually know who. But we are scheduled again on Thursday at the same time. I will come and get you if you are still here then."

Taylor handed the headphones back to him and took a deep breath. "Thank you." He nodded and rose. Angelica slipped her hand into his almost automatically and leaned into him. "At least you know they're all right."

"Where could he have gone?" Taylor asked

"Well, they left in a hurry," Angelica surmised. "Maybe he went back to clear the way for them to return."

"I don't think they'll go back." Taylor shook his head. "It's something else. They have too much notoriety right now, and wild claims like what we were hearing on the news have a tendency to attract strange people who *want* the rumors to be true. Or they want to prove it for the sake of fame. Or they're trying to find a way to make some quick cash..."

"Money!" Angelica snapped her fingers, seizing on the idea. "That's it, then. If they're being compensated from the government, then maybe he went back to take care of the paperwork."

Taylor nodded, still half distracted as he led the way to the door. He paused a moment, his hand on the knob. "I'm glad you were here with me."

Angelica smiled, reaching past him to open the door for them. "Me t—"

The explosion came as a complete surprise.

Chapter 19

I f there had been windows in the building, they would've blown out. The explosion was near enough to rattle Taylor's teeth. Angelica hovered behind him. He could feel the fear emanating off her in waves, yet she'd stood with him, hands clenching and unclenching while one of Olaf's men reported what they thought had happened. She'd surprised him, the steel core coming to the fore when the threat came.

Because of me, he realized. *Because she wants to protect me, as much as I want to protect her.*

It was a heady thought. And somewhat terrifying to a man who wasn't used to depending on anyone. Especially since his life had blown up over these past months.

"This isn't a single assassin," Olaf was saying, translating the frantic report. The man speaking had turned about twelve shades of pale. He was just a kid, barely old enough to shift. He spoke in a rapid patter that would have been near impossible to follow had Taylor known the language. He was impressed Olaf got anything out of it at all.

"How many?" Taylor asked, already mentally cataloguing what he knew of the numbers of possible defenders the compound held. Could they withstand a serious assault?

"This is a unified effort of several, maybe more than several men." Olaf spoke rapidly to the man and translated again. "They parked a car at the gate and then detonated it. That was the explosion. There might have been extra fuel involved to make such a big noise. The gate is gone and they're shooting..."

Taylor could hear it now, the soft popping that echoed through the jungle. The usual calls and counter- calls of the insects and small creatures had silenced. But the small-arms fire grew progressively louder. Getting closer.

"Taylor?" Angelica stood with her fingers curled around his upper arm, fingers digging into the flesh a little. Her entire body shook with tension.

"What arms do you have for self-defense?" Taylor demanded, covering her hand with his, trying to convey that no matter what they *had* this. They would be safe somehow.

"We prefer to hunt as tigers but we do have weapons, mostly for emergencies. There is already a large number of us on their way to the breach. They're carrying everything we have."

"I'm on my way," Taylor promised, and to his surprise Olaf nodded and translated that to the other. He'd actually expected some protest, that he would have to fight for the right to stand with them. But instead both men ran off into the night, trusting him to follow.

"Taylor..."

He turned to her, taking her face in his hands. "This is what I do, Angelica. I was trained for it—I have a lot of experience with it. I have to go."

Angelica nodded. Her eyes were over-bright with unshed tears. She was working hard to be brave, but she'd cry after he left. Heart breaking, wishing he could do anything other than put her through this, Taylor took her in his arms and looked into her eyes. "I'm sorry," he said, bending his head so that his forehead touched hers, so that he could look her in the eyes so close it was like falling forever into their depths. "I'm sorry for ever getting angry. For ever making you sad. For everything I didn't do and should have done. I love you, and I always will."

Angelica lay her hand on his jaw and lifted her face to kiss him.

It felt too much like kissing her goodbye.

Don't get hurt, sweetie. I promise I won't either.

Taylor sought absolution in her tear-bright eyes, staring at her a long moment before he physically had to tear himself from her side.

Taking a deep breath he threw himself down the path full speed, running toward the gunfire and whatever terror awaited him.

Awaited all of them. He felt them in the darkness, the others running with him. They came from all sides, men and women. Tigers. Every one with a common purpose, fighting their way through the jungle to defend what was theirs.

Some might never come back.

I can't afford to think like that.

We *can't afford to think like that.*

So they ran, man and tiger both, two souls united in one body with a common goal.

Defend the mate.

Defend the mate.

ANGELICA COULD HEAR screams in the darkness and she wrapped her arms around herself and shuddered. The idea that Taylor was running *into* that made her feel like she would never be warm again. She stood on the path in front of the building, hearing the computers humming behind her, and wondered where she would go. Where were the others, the ones who weren't going to fight? Certainly not here.

I should find them. Be with the rest. That way Taylor will know where to find me when this is over.

It seemed such a useless thought, to go hide, acting the coward, when she should be with the rest. Surely there was something she could do? She took a cautious step on the darkened path, hoping she could remember the way back to the center of the compound.

"We have been through this before," a calm voice behind her said.

Angelica put a hand to her mouth and tried not to scream as she whirled, nearly falling off the path into the bushes. "Oh!" Her heart pounded in her throat. "Helga. I'm sorry."

"No, child. I owe the apology; I didn't realize I was not heard. I came to check on you and Taylor. Where is he?"

Angelica pointed in the direction of the popping sounds, thinking how each innocent little pop was a bullet that could be tearing through him at any moment. She swallowed hard. *No.* He was too professional for that. They wouldn't take him so easily.

Helga nodded. "He's a brave man," she acknowledged, "but perhaps not wise. The two of you are the goal of these men. We cannot protect him if he insists on being at the forefront of that battle."

Her words broke through the dam she'd been trying so hard to erect since she knew Taylor would have to leave. She'd realized it the moment she'd seen the fireball over the trees that he would leave her behind. Taylor Mann. Hero. "I am so very sorry that we brought this on you and your people." Angelica began wiping away the tears that started to run in hot rivulets down her cheeks. "I am so..."

"I understand your guilt." Helga placed a gentle hand under her chin, raising her head that they might see eye to eye. "But it is misplaced and ill-timed. Men and women are firing guns at one another even as we speak. Cats are entering the fray with bared fangs and unsheathed claws. There will be blood, there will be pain, and there will be death. And those who survive will need attention. We have few medical professionals, and a small... how do you say the word...clinic? We need you to help, to be strong, not to cower and wallow in guilt."

Guilty as charged. Angelica swallowed hard, swiping at tears with the back of her hand. "I'm sor—" She laughed a little, a touch ruefully. No apologies. Right. She could do this. She lifted her chin, feeling the strength coming back into limbs a moment ago she doubted could support her. "Yes, I understand, and you're right—I shouldn't. Tell me where to set up. I'll start preparing for the injured."

Helga nodded, her eyes alight with approval. "Excellent." She took Angelica's shoulder and turned her so that she was facing away from the direction she'd been going. The older woman pointed to a dim opening through the trees. "Follow the path there, down the hill. There is large building there with many lights. The staff do not speak English, but all know you are a doctor."

It wasn't the first time she would work with a staff with a shaky command of the language, but it was daunting all the same. "Olaf said something about someone learning English who could translate for me?"

"She went with the rest." Helga stood and thought for a moment. "I'll come and translate." She smiled at Angelica's reaction. "I might be an elder, but I can look inscrutable and aloof later." She laughed a little. "Besides, advanced age lends a certain gravitas to one's words. I should think I would be obeyed quickly, save some time."

Angelica nodded and placed her hand on the elder's arm and took another breath. She said a quick prayer for Taylor and turned to head down the beaten path to the building that served as a clinic. She moved at a slow jog, wishing that she could go faster, that she had the eyes of the cat to see unseen obstacles in the dark. Helga fell into step behind her. Angelica didn't miss the significance of that. Instead of the acolyte following the elder, the elder followed the doctor. For this part of the journey, Angelica would be the one in charge.

It was a strange and heady feeling. Fear receded. Something else replaced it. A certain calm, the assurance that this at least she knew how to do. Here she could be of service. She could matter.

"I understand you shifted earlier to run from that man," Helga said from behind her. Surprisingly, the older woman kept pace with her easily and didn't even sound winded.

"I did."

"I should warn you to not shift again. Until we discover the location of your inner beast, it becomes progressively dangerous and likely that you might not be able to change back."

"You mean, spend the rest of my life as a lioness?" Angelica called over her shoulder.

"Precisely."

Angelica raised an eyebrow and pictured it. A lioness in a jungle... would that really be all that bad?

The lights from the clinic showed in front of her. It was a large building, the largest she'd seen on the compound, and was at the base of the hills. That made sense: if someone was injured it would be easier to get them downhill rather than up. There were other lights off to the left. The compound proper, she guessed. Somehow she'd come full circle.

She heard a wet thud behind her and turned as another explosion lit the sky. She covered herself, cringing away from the blast, even though it was still too far away for there to be any fallout. When she looked up, she was alone.

"Helga?" she called, but Helga was gone.

Surely she's behind me somewhere...

"HELGA?" Angelica screamed, turning, preparing to go back. In a single bright white flash, the world came to a stunning conclusion and Angelica was no longer in it.

It was followed by the feeling of falling.

She caught a glimpse of worn leather boots before the world went black.

Chapter 20

G unfights were all the same when you got down to it. Men rushing at other men, weapons belching death, howls of rage, screams of hate, shoots of pain, and cries of loss. Taylor worked in a vacuum of that sound. Bullets tore through the trees beside him, shining in the reflected light of the burning car.

He grabbed a rifle someone flung to him, his ears bright—tiger ears hearing the clack of the bullet loading in the chamber. He pointed at a group and gestured with his hand in the direction he needed them to go. They moved under his command as smoothly as if they'd been doing it for years, and dropped down the edge of the ravine to circle around and come at the enemy's flank. He lay still, waiting, then heard the resounding echoes of his erstwhile squad pelting the enemy from the side. Then he rose, half crouched, fired, and made way for one of their own coming back to him.

A woman raced back, limping heavily, rifle in hand, and lay the weapon at his feet. Blood had soaked the cloth at her shoulder, but she smiled at him from a dirt-smeared face, and headed back to the compound as fast as she was able. Another arrived to take up her gun and rejoin the battle.

Around him the battled raged savagely. He aimed, shot, reloaded. Repeat.

Then suddenly it was over.

In a single heart-stopping moment, the noise ceased. No rifles fired, no fresh screams echoed in the greenery. For just a moment, the world held its breath and waited. Taylor rose from the crouch, rifle trained ahead of him. He heard the sounds of engines in the distance, vehicles

driving away, kicking up gravel and dirt as they tore through the back-
roads.

There was a shout. Taylor didn't understand the words. Another.
Olaf appeared in the night, his smile as bright at the full moon. "They
are gone!" he cried. "We scared them off—we beat them!"

It didn't make sense. None of it did.

"Why would we scare them off?" Taylor asked the night.

"Because we outnumbered them and we are without fear," Olaf
shouted, the pride in his voice raising a cheer from those around him
who likely had no idea what he'd just said. Taylor recognized the brava-
do that came from adrenaline and smiled. Let the man enjoy this day.
Others would come. He lowered the rifle and flexed his back.

"Set guards here for tonight," he said, reaching out to touch Olaf's
shoulder, drawing him back from his visions of glory to the here and
now. "Someone to watch the gate until daylight, when it can be re-
paired."

Olaf smiled and actually saluted him before giving orders to the
group. Two men and a woman offered to stay behind.

The battle, though short, hadn't been without loss. There were several casualties. The heart and blood of ancient Vikings were no substitute for experience and training. Two of the defenders lay dead, six
more were being tended for bullet wounds. Once the bullets were removed shifting would close any open holes instantly, but infections
were universal in man and beast, so ideally they needed to be cleaned
first. Taylor had transformed too many times while injured in the last
months and had fought the effects of it after South America. If he could
spare the same here, then so much the better.

He gave orders to that effect. There was some protest, but this was
a people unused to these kinds of injuries. In the end they nodded, urg-
ing their comrades to wait on shifting until they could return to the
clinic, warning against foreign objects under the skin while shifting and
the potential damage it could do.

This would be done under general anesthetic, meaning that the wounds had to be packed until the patient could shift. Battlefield first aid administered, the injured were distributed among the well to carry them back to where they might receive medical treatment. Taylor carried an injured man in his arms to the makeshift clinic and set him down on one of the cots set in the triage area.

"Where's Angelica?" He'd expected to see her there, but when he looked around at the busy staff her bright eyes and dark hair were nowhere to be found. Olaf translated. Answers were sparse. There were more pressing needs than his missing fiancée. His questions were generally ignored, the staff buried in blood, intent on doling out enough painkillers to keep everyone calm. One young attendant simply shrugged and continued on her way.

Olaf looked at Taylor and shook his head.

"Well, she *is* a doctor; did no one think to ask her to help out?" If they were so pissed about the invasion and holding her and, by extension, him to blame for it, there was going to be no end of trouble. Taylor's body was rigid in anger by the time he tracked down the man acting as a doctor, the one tasked with pulling out the bullets. He caught him between patients, holding a long instrument freshly sterilized in one hand, about to administer what passed for surgery on the patient lying unconscious before him. He spat out a long string of words without looking up. Taylor didn't speak the language, but it was easy to tell that most of that dialog wasn't exactly acceptable in most workplaces.

Olaf blanched a little at the tirade and turned to translate, his shoulders slumping with weariness now that the adrenaline had burned out of his system. "He said Elder Helga went to ask her to help, but that she'd refused to come."

"Refused?" Taylor stepped back without realizing it. "She would never refuse."

Olaf shrugged. "They said she never came, and they really could use her right now." It was obvious that by now Olaf was tired of playing translator, and his opinion of Angelica had shifted somewhat after this last bit of information. He seemed irritated and turned away, making it clear that he was done.

Taylor stared at him a moment and then took off out the door. Anyone who knew Angelica knew she'd be the first one here. Someone was lying. She'd been here and turned away. Or something else. Fear suddenly gripped his stomach.

She was missing.

He raced down the road, then turned and headed back up the hill, but stopped and thought a moment. In the light of the medical building there seemed to be a clearing on the other side. From here it looked like there might be a path. A shorter way to get to the room he'd shared with Angelica. He chose this route, jogging easily up the trail, cat eyes giving him the ability to see what he might have missed otherwise—a branching of the path, a lesser used footpath that led back toward where he thought the computer shed might be if he had his directions correct.

Which was, of course, where he'd left her.

He ran along its length, praying that by some miracle she would still be there.

In his haste he stumbled over what he should have seen. A body half-concealed in the foliage, long ferns covering her face, the sickly smell of blood clinging to her clothes. He fell heavily next to her, stunned for a moment. Then realizing that it was a body, still warm, that he was touching, he shouted though he knew no one would hear. Not from here.

"OLAF!" His fingers tore at the leaves, brushing them away from her face.

There was so much blood.

He needed help. Someone. Anyone. His own throat closed, fear and anxiety making it impossible to get the sound out. In desperation he asked the cat.

Do you think you can do it?

I will try.

The tiger's roar torn from his hybrid throat ripped through the jungle and filled the valley. Faces appeared in doorways and up and down the path. People came running, Olaf with them.

Taylor was on one knee, cradling the fallen woman in his arms when they reached him. It wasn't Angelica. He handed her to them, careful to brace Helga's head, to keep her from further injury. She was still bleeding from her skull, her matted hair tumbling around her face. Her breathing was shallow and erratic. It sounded wet and somehow wrong. She smelled... like she was bleeding inside her body, too.

"Get her to the clinic!" Taylor yelled. Many hands turned to carry the old woman to help, but the eyes that belonged to those hands turned balefully to Taylor. He felt their suspicion. The growing anger.

"Do they think *I* did that?" Taylor asked Olaf.

"No," he said curtly as they took the woman away. "They think you're responsible."

He didn't have time for this. While strangers condemned, the love of his life was gone. Missing. If one woman had been hurt and left to die, so too could another. But the path was empty, and he had no sense of her being near. The tiger couldn't scent her.

She was gone.

Taylor spun and ran. Behind him were shouts. Questions. They wanted to know what had happened, how he had found Helga. He could talk to them later. Right now he needed to find Angelica. He ran the rest of the way to his room. Angelica wasn't there.

Somehow he'd known she wouldn't be.

She would have come at my call.

Taylor stood a moment, chest heaving, heart racing. Everything inside of him lost.

What if she's dead?

The tiger didn't answer. He needed to look for her. Maybe she was simply lying unconscious somewhere. The jungle around the camp was thick. She could have been just off the path and no one would have ever known. He returned to the trail. Eyes spotted him and were averted. Tongues whispered words he couldn't understand. Two men were dead. An Elder fought for her life. None of this violence had been part of their lives before he and his mate had come.

Taylor roared again. It was a plea, a searching call, a man—no, beast—seeking his mate. Seeking his other when surrounded by enemies. It was call of wild desperation for the one he loved.

It was answered by silence.

Echoing silence.

The silence of the dead.

Chapter 21

Taylor knew there was a limited number of vehicles in the compound. So far, the only things around with a combustion engine included the car Olaf had used to get them and an old pickup. He expected there to be more somewhere, but from what he'd seen there really hadn't been a need for too many vehicles. He'd thought he'd seen another, a flatbed with some rust issues, but it was long gone. Taylor and Olaf crammed into the car along with three others. There was some confusion for a moment about whose clothing was flung where, but it was sorted out by the time dawn broke. Six more jumped into the back of the pickup and a half-dozen shifted back again when they heard about Angelica being taken.

The entire group was on the road as the first streams of light broke over the trees. They drove behind a pair of tigers. Olaf said they were husband and wife, that they had led the hunters as trackers for decades. They streaked down the road now as fast as tigers could go, an impressive sight in the early morning dawn, two magnificent beasts, low to the ground, moving with a grace equal to nothing else alive. For a moment Taylor envied them their freedom and wished he were out there, doing something more active to bring back the love of his life rather than just sitting and jolting over the dirt track that led out of the compound into the world. To call it a road at all just proved how little Taylor had been in jungles. It was a rutted, worn path of packed dirt that sprouted small green patches of sprouts when the traffic let up.

There was, believe it or not, a T-juncture ahead, which surprised him. It indicated there was actually somewhere else to go in this bloody, forsaken jungle. Their trackers took the fork to the right without hesitation.

Trust them.

I'm trying.

The enemy had who knew how long of a head start on them, but the road was too treacherous for them to gain time. This at least would work in their favor. With any luck the group they were chasing would take the road too quickly for the conditions, impatient and unsure on ground they'd only traversed once before. If they rushed their vehicles would be trashed, and then the pursuit would come to a crashing halt.

It was a positive thought. Olaf pointed out that there were no gas stations out here for repairs and the nearest refueling was 20 miles away, adding his own optimism to the discussion. Even that particular service station was a remote outpost for the occasional hunter or hikers. Most of the time, it wasn't even open.

In the distance, a form appeared on the horizon. The blur shifted and refocused as the inner cat enhanced his vision. It wasn't unlike adjusting binoculars, only without having to hold anything to your face or fiddle with the dials.

Thank you.

Find her.

Taylor was surprised at the cat's mournful plea. He sounded scared. But at least he could see what he'd been staring at now.

"What is that?" Olaf asked, squinting through the dusty windshield and pointing at the form ahead.

"Tiger," Taylor said softly. "One of yours, female, right ear is down, white muzzle, one white foot on the left front."

"Sounds like Ingrid," Olaf said, gritting his teeth and hitting the accelerator a little as the tigers streaking ahead picked up the pace upon sighting their comrade. The vehicle responded with a jolt that rattled everyone's teeth. No one so much as complained.

The lone tiger ran toward them. As she drew near it was obvious that she was exhausted and in pain. She ran past the two in front without hesitation. Olaf frowned and hit the brakes hard enough that Taylor had to throw his hand against the dash to steady himself. The tiger paused at the door of the car. She began to shift, the painful, bone-breaking shift Taylor knew too well and only now realized that he hadn't experienced in days. *When did that start to not hurt?*

When you stopped fighting me.

She appeared then to them, a woman in her early thirties, brilliant blond hair, her body lean to the point of being very thin. A woman from the truck ran up to them with a robe to drape over the woman's back. Although Taylor didn't know the words, he guessed from the nod and weary smile that she was thanking their benefactor. She turned back to Olaf, addressing her comments to the occupants within. Her words were few, but from the way Olaf's face paled what had been said was more than sufficient to add a slump to his shoulders. He glanced at Taylor with pained eyes.

"She said a car is up ahead, much blood."

"Blood? What kind of blood? Whose blood? What did you see?"

Remember when you were the other memory—her cat saw it, not her. She only knows impressions like you used to.

When did the cat get wiser than him?

Taylor gritted his teeth in frustration. Why did no one else have the level of understanding of their cat that he needed them to have right now? "Is the car on this road?" he asked as calmly as he could, going with the basics and what was important.

Olaf translated, and she shook her head. Olaf listened for a bit and turned to Taylor. "She said it is off the road in the trees. It..." He turned to the woman and asked a question. She nodded. "It rolled. Many times."

"Can they find it?" He pointed to their guides.

"Yes." Of this Olaf had no doubt.

"All right, get her in the truck and let her rest. Tell her...tell her I'm grateful for her help."

Olaf smiled and translated. The look she gave him was even, but not angry. "She says," Olaf translated as she spoke, "nothing good comes from the outside."

"I'll try not to take that personally," Taylor said, nodding.

Olaf signaled the pair in front and they loped off in search of the car.

It was off the road far enough that they might not have spotted it at all. It had flipped and rolled several times, coming to rest at the bottom of a ravine, suspended by a mass of thick vines.

Taylor looked down at the wreckage. There was no way to get in there. He looked at the people with him; they all had the same thought. Even a tiger couldn't get down that steep drop to the car that was half-suspended over the river.

I can.

Are you sure?

I can. Trust me.

Taylor took a deep breath and pulled the shirt off. He dropped the pants and shifted as he bent over. There was no pain anymore, no lingering snap of bone, no agonizing transition, just an easy flow into the tiger. Those shifters around him jumped back.

They fear me?

No. They don't understand the embrace. They still fight inside.

Taylor stretched and reached the edge of the embankment. His razor-sharp claws dug into the loam and the dirt. He turned and allowed himself to slide, reaching a root, digging in, suspended by one claw over the precipice.

He kicked out his rear leg and looked down. There was a large rock jutting out halfway down the ridge. Watching the rock, he let go of the root and slid down the edge of the fall. He dug into the heavy dirt to slow his descent, but he couldn't stop it. His rear paw hit the rock hard. He balanced on the outcropping and breathed a sigh of relief.

The rock gave way and he slid again. There was nothing else to grab, nothing to stop the fall to the bottom, and there was no instant healing from a fall like this. He spun on his back, flipping over to reach for a low-hanging branch. He caught it in his paw, but only the end, and it broke under his weight and reached up to strike his face, and he had nothing left to grab before he plummeted over the precipice.

He caught the branch in his mouth and bit down hard. The sudden stop jarred his head and nearly tore out his teeth. But he was hanging from the branch by his mouth, which was better than dying. Heart thundering in his chest he flexed his neck, his entire body weight dependent on that thin branch, praying it would hold for just a little longer. He dragged himself up, closer to the tree. He reached out, but it was beyond his reach.

Taylor dug his rear paws into the soft dirt, as deep as he could. He braced his front paws under him. The branch in his mouth began to fray under the assault of his razor-sharp teeth. When his rear legs were in as far as he could take them, he pushed off and let go of the branch. Scrabbling paws threw dirt down the crevasse, and his body began to fall. In desperation, he stretched in a single last-ditch effort and sank his claws into the bole of the tree.

He pulled as hard as he could and grabbed it with the other claw. This tree, at least, held. He pulled himself up and embraced the trunk like a long lost lover and took a moment to breathe.

Told you I could do it.

He turned. The car was even with his gaze. She wasn't in it.

On the other hand, there were two men trapped in the twisted metal. Both dead. Bodies contorted, a broken branch speared one body, ending his life as effectively as a javelin. They'd died from the wreck then. No claw marks. Nothing to indicate that Angelica was to blame.

Taylor breathed a sigh of relief.

He sat back, lips parted as he lifted his head to test the wind, aware that his perch was precarious as he stopped to think. There was no scent of her on the wind. She'd gotten away. He took a closer look. Her clothing was there, lying on the door. She'd left as a lion. Likely she'd changed while they were driving. Suddenly finding themselves with an angry, fully grown lioness in the back of an old Buick was too much, and they'd lost control. But even under such duress, she hadn't killed.

But she'd shifted. And the words of the elders came back to him. She might not be able to change back. She might not remember who he was, who *she* was. Taylor pulled himself up the tree. He sprang from the uppermost branch to the ground, with enough momentum to dig in and claw his way back up to the road. It was a painful ascent, made more difficult by the stress and strain he'd put on muscles he didn't know he had. He lay in the sun, every inch of his body on fire.

You did well. We need to find her now.

They will help?

I need to tell them what I saw...

Taylor choked and couldn't breathe. The air burned in his lungs but it wouldn't come. He couldn't breathe, he...

With a great ragged gasp, he tore the wind back into his lungs and fell again. He'd changed without realizing he was going to, taken by surprise.

No. Worse. Only part of him had shifted.

Sorry.

He would need to discuss this with the tiger later. He needed them to work as a cohesive whole. The tiger couldn't just initiate the transformation like that without warning. He shook his head, still a little dizzy from the unexpectedness of coming together in pieces. He cleared his throat, just managing to choke out the words. "She's not in there."

Olaf was staring at him in horror. He wasn't the only one.

"She's shifted," he managed to choke out, unsure if he'd been clear or not in his previous words.

"How can you... you're like the elders..."

"NEVER MIND THAT. We have to find her."

They backed away from him. Scared? Taylor wasn't sure what to make of that. Olaf stared out at the precipice. At the dense underbrush and trees that blocked out the sun. "It's a big jungle, my friend."

"Yes. But in the whole jungle there is only one African lion. How hard can it be?"

He didn't wait for an answer. Let them follow him or not. He wouldn't rest until her found her. Taylor rose and ran back down the road. If she wasn't in there, she was thrown free when the men panicked maybe. She might have left the car before the car left the road, so she should be...

There. Her smell.

FIND THE MATE.

DONE.

Over.

The jungle was vast. There was nothing that could hold against a lioness. Nothing.

Rabbit. Drives to the side, not straight.

No one was looking for her here. No one would kill innocent people to catch her here. Let Griselda come. Let her send a hundred men next time. They would never find her. The jungle was too wild, too vast. She dodged around a grouping of trees, noting them idly as she passed.

Kashmir maple. Strong, resilient. Home to bird nests, strong branches.

It had all been too much. The strain had been taking a toll on her and Taylor since they'd left Africa. It had torn them apart and whenever it looked like they could reconcile... everything had blown up all over again. Now his family had been routed, and she'd told him that it wasn't his fault because, quite simply, it wasn't.

It was hers.

If she'd been able to control the change, if those damned exercises had worked, if she'd worked a little harder... but no, they'd been at each other's throats. What had been beautiful between them had slowly and inexorably been wrecked. There was no salvation. No going back.

She couldn't do it anymore. And there was no reason to.

Vixen. Cunning. Hides easily, runs quick, but in short bursts. Likes to run in a circle.

She loved Taylor. Adored him. But he was in danger because of her, too. So far he was another of a mythological group that had a strange power that people envied. But she was the product of a repeatable scientific process. She was the promise that anyone could be a shifter, that anyone's DNA could be cut and sewn and rearranged until they were all cats or dogs or horses.

This was the only one that worked. All the other attempts failed.

Angelica paused to get her bearings. She heard the cries of the wounded at the encampment. They were still dealing with the aftermath of the battle. She knew men and women had been hurt, maybe even killed. And the elder... oh, God, the elder, assaulted and left to bleed and all because Griselda wanted the secret. The way to be a shifter.

Her fault. More people suffering because of her.

She'd become a doctor to ease suffering. She'd wanted to make things better. Even now she fought the urge to go down, to lend her skills where they might help, might ease things for those people, too. But the very act of returning to the compound would put more people in danger. Again. Because of her. Because she happened to be the missing link.

Incompatible DNA attributes are not the only indicators of a successful splice to the gene. There are other factors which preclude adaptation necessary to achieve symbiosis.

So instead Angelica ran into the jungle, blindly, searching for nothing else but a place to be, away from the stress and bloodshed and insanity that her life had become. The form of the large cat made it easy to travel paths she never could have as a human. Leafy fronds that would have slowed her progress slid over the back as she slipped beneath them. Wide paws gave her purchase, balance where she would have had none. The beauty, the grace of the lion was hers to embrace. Here she was no klutz, tripping over her own feet. Here she moved simply, easily. Not perfectly, no. The lion was meant for a different climate, a different altitude even. But here, she could learn to adapt. Wasn't that what being a shifter was? An individual who embraced the adaptations necessary to survive?

Eventually she found a raging river that tore through the landscape, slowly destroying everything in its path. She followed the raging waters for a time, but a natural aversion to the fast-flowing water kept her back from its banks. In time she found a place where a rivulet branched off, a small side stream where the rushing waters calmed. Here, where the waters nourished and fed the soil, she lay down and drank.

The smell of rabbit. It was here recently.

Angelica froze. It was the same singsong voice that she'd developed over the years to remember the endless parade of medical knowledge she'd had to memorize. The one she thought she'd lost until today, when it had surfaced again after she'd left the wreck of the car smoldering in the underbrush. But that voice had never said anything that wasn't a catalog of facts. And what about earlier? The words had made no sense.

'Compatible DNA attributes?' What the hell does that even mean?

The physiological aspects of the addition of the RNA strand is not as important as the psychological propensity to have an alternative mental outlet for the change, not only physical.

WAIT. Angelica leapt to her feet in shock, the lioness shaking water droplets from her coat, pacing and frantic on the riverbank. *YOU'RE my inner beast?*

There is no requirement for a 'beast' to be beastly.

She sat down heavily on her haunches, suddenly overwhelmed and completely at a loss. *So the others, the ones that Dr. Johns experimented on... they died because...*

They did not have the psychological fractions to which the altered state of physical—

They didn't have an inner beast, Angelica interrupted, finding her own thoughts in the morass of input that was clearly not her own. She lay down, panting a little in the heat of the sun, trying to process this.

They didn't have an inner beast.

Angelica lay by the stream in wonder. It had been there all along, in plain sight, and it had been there long before her cells were changed. The inner beast was a scientific know-it-all.

Somewhat offensive.

She would have laughed if she could, but she rolled over in the dappled sunlight and stretched her legs to the sky, staring at her wide paws with a wonder, an acceptance she had not previously found. This too was part of her. This was normal. She flexed her claws, seeing them splay before retreating, sheathing again within the pads of her feet. This was where she belonged. Here was safe, and moreover, in staying here everyone else would become safe; safe from the people hunting her. Safe from killing and explosions and running and looking over her shoulder. Safe from...

Taylor.

She sighed and flopped back, letting the ferns that grew along the bank cover her. Safe from Taylor? Taylor was her safe place. He was her anchor, her rock. That thought brought her up short. To hide here was to be gone from him.

No. It's Taylor.

Angelica lifted her head. A large, muscular tiger with intense eyes stood on a rise above her, looking down. He didn't move. It might have been him, but in that light...

It is Taylor. Can you not smell him?

Angelica smiled, feeling her own lips curl back in an expression of what she guessed was feline satisfaction. She wondered if she could do as he had done: could she manipulate part of her to change back? Could she find the human again?

In response her legs grew, straightened, her hips reset and re-formed, her body reshaped and moved and she looked down and this time she did laugh. A genuine laugh. The transition hadn't hurt at all.

There is no reason it should. If the shift is an evolutionary construct, then the evolution would favor a process that did not cause pain. It only hurts when the muscles contract and battle the morphosis, if the change is not fought, it's painless.

Taylor loped down the hillside and changed as he walked toward her. It was like watching a liquid flowing from cat to man, mid-step, smooth, as if it weren't the most unbalancing thing he could do.

Okay, now that *is impressive.*

"Just when I think I've caught up to you," she said in shy wonder at the way his muscles gleamed in the sunlight, "you raise the bar."

He knelt down beside her, indeed fully man. Her pulse leaped as his fingers reached to cup her cheek, her jaw. His voice was tender, his voice rough with emotion. "I was afraid I lost you." The words were almost a sob. He'd been frantic. For *her.* It was a heady thought. Something that she'd known he could be capable of, somewhere, in the recesses of her mind, but that she'd forgotten in the last few weeks.

She leaned into the caress. "I had the inner beast all along." She let her lips whisper across his palm. Soft kisses, tasting the salty sweat on his skin. "I just didn't know that it wasn't so beastly." She finished her own change, one that had halted uncomfortably with more fur than skin, and rose to stand in front of him, with a shy awareness that as much as he was male, she was female. Her breasts jutted toward him, nipples peaked and hard. When he wrapped her in his arms he held onto her for dear life.

Yes, fully male. Fully male and wanting her. She pressed that part of herself to him there, letting him know that she desired more than comfort, but that she desired him. Just him.

His hand cupped her hip, pressing her closer. There was no doubt that he felt the same way.

Breathing ragged, he cleared his throat and spoke. "The entire village is looking for you," he said into her ear.

She understood and sighed. This wasn't the time or place for a proper reunion. Here they'd only just found each other and she wanted, as much as he wanted, the union that would consummate this moment. Only, there was a certain responsibility to let them know that she was all right. That they could cease searching.

I'm not going back, though. I'll let them know I'm all right, but after that we leave. We can go find somewhere else maybe. Another jungle. Farther from here. Someplace where a person...no, a lion can get lost and never be found.

Besides, it was a task better done now rather than later. Being found like this would be embarrassing to a certain extent. Especially if they carried out what they both instinctively wanted. Needed.

She shifted her hips against his. Letting him know that she wouldn't forget this moment even if it needed to be interrupted. "I want..." Her words were wistful as she stepped back.

He nodded, his expression holding a certain wonder, a trace of hope. "You'll be okay?" He reached to tangle his fingers in her hair, to draw her close for a kiss that was an eternity and somehow still not long enough. She responded with all the pent-up passion and want and desire that had been suppressed for far too long.

She drew back, laughing. "I've never been more okay in my life," she replied, and shifted back to the lioness, surprising him. Had he truly not expected it? Had he thought maybe they'd travel back to the compound on foot, human, because in his mind it was still too dangerous for her to change? She would show him then. Maybe she didn't have

Taylor's smoothness but it didn't hurt, at least not as much as it had in the past. That, at least, was something to be grateful for. She leaped into the jungle and vanished among the fronds, trusting him to follow.

Behind her she heard Taylor call her name, several times, a hint of panic in his voice. He had been caught unprepared after all. He would learn. Let him see that she could be trusted with this. That she was all right after all.

A moment later she heard his roar. Dominant. Masculine. Right on her tail. Angry. When he caught her, there would be hell to pay.

Let him rage. She needed to be true to herself. Laughing inwardly with joy, having finally come into her own, Angelica raced low to the ground. She had the entire jungle before her. Maybe she didn't need to leave Taylor behind completely to find the peace she'd craved. Maybe things could work out—for the woman and lion both—after all.

Chapter 22

She ran forever, for a year, for a lifetime. It felt that way, even though she knew it was just a short time. She ran away, never toward, always away. She was aware that she needed to return to the compound, or at least find another shifter from the community to let them know that she was all right, that she was leaving. But now that she'd shifted, she was in no hurry to do so. The freedom she enjoyed now was calling to her. Let her put some miles of jungle between her and the world. Let her enjoy this moment. With each passing fall of her feet she gained on the small apartment; she gained on those set out to catch her, she gained on Mrs. Petrov and the Mann family and all the rest in the sleepy village who gave up all they'd worked so hard for because of her. She gained on the elders at the camp. She gained on all the grief and guilt and shame.

Taylor was close behind her, more suited to this jungle than she was. Lions preferred open plains with tall grass. She was on his ancestral home turf now, so he should have beaten her twice. What hadn't he? Why did he hold back? Perhaps he was falling behind to extend their time together as well. Was he agreeing with her? Did he also feel that going home by the long way around was all right, even preferable?

Doubtful; he smells angry.

The lion was right. She'd scared him, changing like that. He didn't understand. She hadn't taken the time to explain. She probably should have.

I didn't because I didn't want another argument. What if he'd told me no? I couldn't take that chance. No. Let him see who I am. Let him taste the freedom that I do right now. Let him find understanding.

It was a lovely thought, though how likely it was she didn't want to contemplate. Thankfully the lion was silent. She didn't need the analytical know-it-all right now.

She ran on for a time, following the river upstream. A muted roar in the distance that wasn't made by an animal spurred her on to move faster. She didn't really know what she was looking for until she stumbled into the center of the very place she hadn't known she was looking for until now.

Here there was another rend in the landscape, another channel dug through the rich soil from relentless water flowing down. But this was different from the stream he'd found her at before. This one had a waterfall. It was ten, maybe fifteen feet high. She stopped there, at the edge of the pool the waterfall had created, and changed back, breathless and exhilarated. She didn't wait for him, but dipped her foot into the soothing, cool water, discovering to her delight that the temperature wasn't too cold after all. She slid off the bank into the depths, and when he was in range she pushed off into the deeper pool at the base of the waterfall and let the fish nibble at her toes.

She stood under the spray, feeling the warm water cascading down between her breasts. The water came only to her waist here. Perfect for rinsing the dirt and sweat from her skin, from her hair.

Taylor shifted on the bank. He didn't look pleased. Well, his face wasn't pleased. There was a part of him that was very pleased, and that part was growing. She focused on that, reminding herself that, regardless of how mad he was, they still at least had that.

In fact *that* was looking rather appealing right now. She licked her lips, savoring the hunger.

"Where..." He opened his arms in confusion. "Where are you running to? The compound is over there." He waved his hand vaguely somewhere off to his left.

"How about here?" she asked, lying back to float, enjoying the feel of the sun on her breasts. She moved her hands in lazy circles so that her body rotated gracefully in a circle. "Does it remind you of anything?"

His eyes were rather focused on her breasts. Apparently, he liked them in the sunshine as well, for possibly different reasons. He nodded, though his expression stayed grim. "The grotto in the Amazon." He shook his head. "Need I remind you that someone out there," he gestured again at the jungle, "attacked the compound last night? They tried to kidnap you. They could still be out there. In fact they probably are. I don't see Griselda—"

She put her feet down and stood to face him. "That's just it. I *don't* see Griselda. Or anyone else. I'm not a complete idiot, Taylor, but can't you at least let me have *this* for a moment? I'm tired of fighting. I'm tired of running. I'm tired of hiding. I just want this. Here. Now. You. Let's just be *us* for ten minutes."

There may have been tears in her eyes, it was hard to tell; the cold crystal clear water tumbling from the waterfall was misting her with a fine spray. She was freezing; the water was not as warm as she'd initially thought, despite the heat of the jungle, and her feet were getting numb.

"Taylor," she begged. She begged with every fiber, every part of her. "Taylor, please. Let's stay here. Just us. It's a big jungle. We can get lost, we can go away, no one has to be hurt again because of us. We can just be... gone. Please? We'll go back and tell everyone we're leaving. They don't have to worry about us anymore. And we make a big show of just... taking off. Only we don't. We just... shift. Live here." She sank so that she was underwater to her chin. It was warmer that way even if she had to blow out some water that tried to go into her mouth. At least he didn't look mad anymore. Sad, yes, but angry?

"You didn't ask me about your kidnappers," he said softly. "The ones in the car."

She closed her eyes and the image of the two men reappeared. "I saw them." She opened her eyes again and looked into his face, pleading for his understanding. "Taylor, I didn't kill them, I swear."

"I know. They died from the car flipping over. I thought...I thought you were in there, that I was going to pull your body from that wreckage."

Angelica swallowed hard. She hadn't thought. It had never even occurred to her at the time that someone would find the car. That they would think the worst. She'd been so intent on getting *away* that she'd thought of nothing else. "I'm sorry. I didn't think." She took a step toward him. "But don't you see? This is what I'm talking about. We can live out here, it's a *jungle*! It can feed us, house us. Please, Taylor, no more deaths for our sake. We can just stay."

"No, Angelica, we can't." He looked at her with eyes weighed down by duty. Responsibility. His dog tags reflected the dying light, a tangible reminder of who he was. Of what he believed in.

She swallowed hard, taking another step toward him, hand out. Still pleading, but knowing it was useless. He needed to go back. And she needed him. "Taylor, I love you, but this...this isn't..."

"Angel—" Taylor stumbled, his eyes growing wide. His back arched as the bullet she hadn't even heard being fired passed through his chest, spraying blood over the pool.

Angelica screamed. She couldn't stop screaming.

Taylor staggered once and fell, landing on his side at the edge of the water, his eyes still wide open and staring.

Chapter 23

D*IVE!*
Angelica was frozen, daring to call her eyes liars. This wasn't real, couldn't be real. He was shot. Taylor was hurt and bleeding out and she didn't have anything to...

DIVE!

Angelica nearly drowned as she was pulled under the water, by a control over her body that quite clearly wasn't her own.

"DAMN YOU TO HELL!" a woman shrieked above her. "I don't need him dead!"

"He moved!" someone protested.

The woman's voice...

"Then find the woman, and if you kill her so help me I will skin you alive, you pathetic little—"

Angelica listened. The voice was distorted by the water; it was muffled, strange.

Vocal frequencies, idiomatic rhythms, and accent. Voice confirmed.

Griselda.

Angelica grabbed the rocks at the base of the waterfall, still underwater. Her lungs began to burn with the effort of holding in the breath she refused to let go. If the inner beast wasn't beastly, then by God and all the saints she would be.

When the lioness exploded from the water with a roar that shook the jungle, the man with the rifle was too shocked to move much less try to fire. The lioness was on him in a moment, landing on him, 600lbs of force on the man's stomach and ribs. Things cracked and gave way.

Third and fourth ribs shattered, internal injuries, possible damage to one lung. With treatment, survivable.

The great claw wrapped around the rifle and flung it backward into the water. The lion looked up, triumphant, only to see Griselda, ten feet away, with pistol aimed not at her but at Taylor's head. "I think he's dead. I can be sure." She cocked the gun. "What do you say? Wanna play? Oh!" She waggled the pistol. "I should probably tell you that your little band is currently being rounded up by my men. Don't expect a rescue. I couldn't have done it without you, you know. On the road they would have had me, but this fun little romp in the jungle? I got to take them out one by one." She smiled, the gun never wavering. "I don't need him if I have you, sweetheart." She smiled. "So, a life for a life?"

A rattling of bushes announced the arrival of another eight of her goons. They had a prisoner. Olaf. They threw him to his knees, naked. The man who'd held him set a boot on his prone body and pointed his rifle down at his head.

Angelica froze. Never taking her eyes off Griselda, she allowed herself to change back. She automatically thought to try to hide her nudity, but refused to be cowed by these people. Instead of lewd comments, she heard only gasps. It was one thing to be told what your prey was; it was another to see it happen.

"Leave him alone."

"You're in no position to give orders." Griselda shook her head, the gun steady. "You didn't even say please."

Angelica stood her ground, hate radiating from her. Never would she have so cheerfully killed another living being as now. She bit back a hundred possible responses, her brain running in every direction, looking for a way out. *I've been so incredibly stupid. Stupid and naïve.*

The silence dragged on too long for the drug lord. Griselda looked at the man who held Olaf, his boot on the man's neck. "Very well. You leave me no choice. Kill that one."

"NO!" Angelica hissed. She swallowed hard. Fought to spit out the final word, when it caught in her throat. "Please."

But while she kept her face on Griselda, the only thing she had to fight with right now was herself. She tried to raise her breasts a little, slide one hip upward, lift a leg, anything to keep their attention away from the rustling in the jungle behind them, or the movement under Griselda's gun.

Be a distraction. It's sexist. It's evil. It's wrong. You can kill all the bastards later. But for now, be a fucking distraction.

"That wasn't so hard, was it?" Griselda laughed. "Just for that, I'll be nice." She glanced over at her man, her gaze triumphant and icy cold. "Kill him quick."

The man leered in Angelica's direction and raised his rifle.

The sudden impact of a young, fully grown male tiger propelled him forward, tripping over the prone form of Olaf and into the rocks. His rifle flew from his grip, hitting the water much in the same place the first one had, and he slumped.

That's Harold.

Griselda fired. The bullet slammed into the ground; Taylor wasn't there. A great tiger reached from behind her and sank his teeth into the back of her shirt and pulled. Griselda tried to get a second shot, but her balance was off. She went down hard as the clearing filled with tigers.

Griselda's men were caught by surprise; their accomplishment in securing the village had made them complacent. They were assaulted from all sides; one got off a shot, but hit nothing. Dozens of angry tigers pinned them to the ground. The noise was deafening. Angelica had never witnessed anything like it—would likely never do so again. The roars as they slammed into their prey, the screams of the men, the snapping of bones.

And while Angelica might have had issues with taking a life, these tigers did not. It was over in moments.

Griselda screamed, a sound of desperation and fury as she twisted away and somehow made it to her feet, her clothing torn and her face bloodied. Angelica saw her rise and followed the movement with her eyes, seeing what no one else had time to.

"TAYLOR, WATCH OUT!"

It was too late for warnings. Taylor had a grip on the woman, but she had produced a knife in her other hand. The pistol fired again, and she heard the ricochet as it caromed off a rock. Griselda tried to stab behind her, aiming to hit Taylor anywhere, but Taylor pulled back and in that motion tumbled them both end over end into the pond.

They fell, hissing and thrashing, at war, tooth to tooth through the very end. They rolled a moment on the water, churning up the still pond as Angelica cried out his name.

Everything felt chaotic. One moment death was knocking on their door, the next death was destroying those around them. The seesaw of this life was killing them.

Angelica watched, unable to tear her eyes away and suddenly knowing the outcome.

It was over in less than a minute. Griselda was, after all, only a woman, and stood no chance against an enraged tiger. Angelica waited for him to surface, holding her breath as he must have been holding his. He only had to let go. But something was wrong. Either he wouldn't or he couldn't. Griselda seemed determined to kill him no matter what happened. Had she taken him to the bottom after all?

"Taylor?" The name was wrenched from somewhere so deep that it left pain in the passing. She stumbled to the edge of the pond, but the surface had grown still. It was as if Taylor and Griselda had been swallowed by the water. Angelica knelt by the shore, looking for her love but seeing nothing. She became aware of others beside her. Harold. Dmitri. Olaf. One of the members of the council in Minnesota. All watching the still waters beneath them. Harold? Dmitri? When had they—

Taylor should be out now. This was too long under water. Way too long.

"TAYLOR!" she screamed. The cry seared her lungs, rang in her head, echoing forever. It was fear and anger and desperation made into a single cry. She sobbed, and from her throat a roar erupted that rivaled her last, a sound that woke the dead and silenced an entire jungle.

A hand shot to the surface. A dozen more reached to capture it. They pulled Taylor's limp body from the watery depths.

"Taylor!" She was on him in an instant, pushing aside helpful hands to engulf him in an embrace that would have done him no good at all, had the lion not come to the fore and taken control.

Lay the victim on his side to drain the water, begin chest compressions, mouth to mouth as indicated.

Angelica was already breathing for him. Harold, seeing what she was doing, jumped in to do the chest compressions, singing under his breath to time the presses. Angelica breathed and put her mouth over Taylor's and exhaled, forcing his chest to rise. It wasn't working; he was going to die. Or he was dead already. She'd lost him. Dammit, she'd lost it. This was all her fault!

He jerked suddenly, his entire body convulsing, his flesh working independent of the mind. The contractions of the stomach forced water out of his lungs and they strained for air, but there was too much left inside to block the way. He'd come to life only to drown after all.

"Hold him!" Angelica shouted, already moving to turn him. "Upside down!"

They all grabbed, lifted, held him as the water drained from his body. When it seemed that there could be no more water inside, she had them set him down again, motioning for Harold to resume the chest compressions. She took a deep breath, the inner cat of hers taking it, too, and they breathed as one into his mouth.

He rose again, this time spluttering and coughing and retching. His arms flew out to scrabble at the dirt as he rid himself of the last of the water and fell back, exhausted.

When he looked up it was with a strange wonder, as he was staring into the face of his brother. "Thanks, brother." His voice was weak, hoarse. He coughed again, violently. It was Angelica who held him until he stopped. Taylor's hand came up to cup her cheek, eyes saying what his mouth could not.

Harold sat back in silent wonder, making no move to hide the tears that escaped the rigid control he'd had for far too long.

It was finally over.

Something settled in Angelica's stomach. Or maybe her heart. The lion inside her acknowledged it as well.

Peace. Or a sense of it, for the first time in a long, long time.

Epilogue

"Why is it, Randall, that when we finally get away after living a nightmare you always show up at our hotel room door?" Angelica gave him a kiss on the cheek by way of welcome as she ushered him into the room.

"Because I'm the one who's always paying for the hotel room?" he ventured to guess.

"Of course," Taylor agreed without getting up. "What, you think we can swing a suite like this on my salary?" He sat on the couch, feet up on the coffee table, ankles crossed, remote pointed at the screen. He'd been trying to decide between two different ball games for the last five minutes and was driving Angelica crazy. She took the remote out of his hand and shut the TV off completely.

"I'm currently between jobs," Angelica reminded Taylor and plopped onto the couch beside him, snuggling in under his arm where she fit so well.

Randall came in, chuckling, and sat in the chair indicated. "You do realize that I have a congressman wondering why half the population of a small town who all fled the country on the heels of a mad general suddenly boarded a plane and flew to Nepal," Randall began. "And why they returned not to Minnesota, but to Canada."

"Wasn't that sweet?" Angelica murmured to Taylor, still smiling for all she was worth. "It was so nice of them to come out to the wedding, even if it was half a world away." She tilted her head to kiss Taylor's chin.

"Wedding?" Taylor and Randall spoke as one.

"Is it our fault that Nepalese weddings aren't recognized in the U.S.?" She looked as sweet and innocent as she knew how. Both men turned to each other.

After a long moment, Randall nodded. "Yeah, that I can use."

Taylor ruffled Angelica's hair. "Yeah, not bad. You think pretty fast, don't you?"

"So, with that taken care of," Randall said, leaning forward in his chair, elbows on his knees, hands clasped in front of him, "is it true Griselda is dead?"

Angelica inhaled sharply. It was a memory she could do very well without.

"Very," Taylor said with a grimace, pulling Angelica closer, letting her know that he understood, that he was still there.

"And her men?"

"Were left to the tender attention of the locals," Angelica said with more than a little bloodthirsty glee, which surprised even her.

This is the thing that surprises you out of all of this?

"Turns out," Taylor added, leaning over to pour some coffee for his boss, "They have an old autonomy clause that was granted to them hundreds of years ago. What happens on their land, stays on their land."

"And currently, a large number of unarmed former drug dealers are staying on their land. I believe that they dealt with them as they thought best," Angelica chimed in.

Randall leaned over to take the offered cup from Taylor. He stirred in a packet of sugar as he spoke. "And from my estimation about six people from your town attended your, uh, wedding."

Taylor nodded. "Yeah. They all wanted to be there, too. It's good to know when people have your back. Seems a shame that we have to have another wedding, just to make it all legal."

"Taylor," Angelica bit her lip, trying to cover for the sudden surge of emotion that his words had given her. "You don't have to take it that far. It's just a cover; I'm fine."

Randall tossed a small object to Taylor. "Seems like you might be needing this after all," he murmured, and sat back to sip his coffee.

"Taylor?"

"I asked Randall to bring this by," Taylor said. "I got this when we got back from Africa, but things got crazy..." He held it in his open palm. It was a small, black velvet box. Angelica looked at Randall and then at Taylor.

"What?"

Oh, shit!

She stared at it, not daring to touch it. Taylor finally leaned forward and opened the lid. Inside was a sparkling promise, a future in a diamond.

"I know we've used it as a cover a couple dozen times. And talked about it so many times to so many people, but somehow we never got around to making it real. To making it official. So I'm asking you for the last time, will you marry me? Officially, I mean."

Angelica threw herself into his arms and knocked them both off the couch. They crashed into the coffee table, but she didn't care. She was crying as he slid the ring onto her finger.

"I mean it," he warned her. "There's going to be a ceremony and everything. You're not getting out if it this time."

She nodded wildly, lifting her hand to stare at the way the diamond caught the light. She could swear her inner lion was purring. If lions actually purred.

"Congratulations." Randall smiled. It was the first genuine smile she'd ever seen from him. "And don't worry about the coffee table—I'll consider it a wedding present."

"Oh, Randall, I'm sorry! I just—" Angelica was gushing and she knew it. Taylor beamed from ear to ear.

"Listen, take a long and happy honeymoon at *your own* expense. But I'm rude enough to interfere in this moment because I want to talk to you about after."

"After?" Angelica and Taylor exchanged glances.

"Unless you found a long-lost treasure in Nepal, you're going to have to work eventually."

"I'll come back as soon as you need me," Taylor promised.

"I'm afraid that won't happen. Don't look so shocked. There have been too many questions about you lately, and I've had to do some pretty heavy lifting just to keep you under the radar. As an agent, your days are done."

"But—"

"However, there is a different division. A brand new one in fact, that I've just begun. It's an off-the record group of international..." There was a polite knock at the door. Randall looked up. "Ah, I expect that's her now. Right on time."

Angelica looked to Taylor, who shrugged.

Randall continued speaking as he went to the door. "I want you both to lead the team," he said over his shoulder.

"Wait, what?"

"Me? I'm a doctor. I don't—"

But Randall was ignoring them. He'd already opened the door. He spoke quietly to the person on the other side and stepped back.

A long-legged girl of about sixteen walked in. She was wearing a short skirt, and a light beige sweater that perfectly set off her ebony skin. She carried herself like Cinderella at the ball, dignified but with a little uncertainty of her place.

She walked in and waved shyly at them both, a brilliant grin splitting her angular face.

"This is your first trainee and teammate, and her name is..."

"CHARRA!" Angelica screamed, the face suddenly clicking in her memory. "CHARRA?"

The girl grinned and nodded. Angelica ran to embrace her, pulling her right off the floor and swinging her around the room in absolute glee.

Taylor turned to Randall. "A team of shifters? Are you crazy?"

"Yes." Randall nodded, watching the women greet each other. "I'm also best man."

Taylor looked at him a long moment and lay a hand on Randall's shoulder. It might have morphed a little bit as he pressed down.

"And get that hairy thing off me..."

THE END

Shifting Desires Series

Book 1: Jungle Heat
Book 2: Jungle Fever
Book 3: Jungle Blaze

Find Lexy Timms:

L exy Timms Newsletter:
http://eepurl.com/9i0vD
Lexy Timms Facebook Page:
https://www.facebook.com/SavingForever
Lexy Timms Website:
http://www.lexytimms.com

Want

MORE READS?

Sign up for Lexy Timms' newsletter
And she'll keep you up to date on new releases,
giveaways and toss some free ARCs and new
books your way!

Sign up for news and updates!
http://eepurl.com/9i0vD

More by Lexy Timms:

TORN BETWEEN TWO WORLDS. And four men.

Sebastian. Toshi. Theo. Kyle.

I thought that plane crash would be the end of my life. Instead, it turned out to be just the beginning.

Now, I'm on a race to find out who—and what—I really am, with four men to help me. Sexy Sebastian who can be a jerk sometimes but actually means well. Kind Theo whose heart is as big as that chest I want to cozy up against. Slick Toshi who is as fierce as he is fun. And Kyle, my best friend for so long, maybe too long.

They will help me find the answers I seek, though only I can take control of my destiny.

And my heart.

FROM BEST SELLING AUTHOR, Lexy Timms, comes a billionaire romance that'll make you swoon and fall in love all over again.

Jamie Connors has given up on men. Despite being smart, pretty, and just slightly overweight, she's a magnet for the kind of guys that don't stay around.

Her sister's wedding is at the foreground of the family's attention. Jamie would be find with it if her sister wasn't pressuring her to lose weight so she'll fit in the maid of honor dress, her mother would get off her case and her ex-boyfriend wasn't about to become her brother-in-law.

Determined to step out on her own, she accepts a PA position from billionaire Alex Reid. The job includes an apartment on his property and gets her out of living in her parent's basement.

Jamie has to balance her life and somehow figure out how to manage her billionaire boss, without falling in love with him.

** The Boss is book 1 in the Managing the Bosses series. All your questions won't be answered in the first book. It may end on a cliff hanger.

For mature audiences only. There are adult situations, but this is a love story, NOT erotica.

"His body is perfect. He's got this face that isn't just heart-melting but actually kind of exotic..."

Lillian Warren's life is just how she's designed it. She has a high-paying job working with celebrities and the elite, teaching them how to better organize their lives. She's on her own, the days quiet, but she likes it that way. Especially since she's still figuring out how to live with her recent diagnosis of Crohn's disease. Her cats keep her company, and she's not the least bit lonely.

Fun-loving personal trainer, Cayden, thinks his neighbor is a killjoy. He's only seen her a few times, and the woman looks like she needs a drink or three. He knows how to party and decides to invite her to over--if he can find her. What better way to impress her than take care of her overgrown yard? She proceeds to thank him by throwing up in his painstakingly-trimmed-to-perfection bushes.

Something about the fragile, mysterious woman captivates him.

Something about this rough-on-the-outside bear of a man attracts Lily, despite her heart warning her to tread carefully.

He groaned. This was torture. Being trapped in a room with a beautiful woman was just about every man's fantasy, but he had to remember that this was just pretend.

Allyson Smith has crushed on her boss for years, but never dared to make a move. When she finds herself without a date to her brother's upcoming wedding, Allyson tells her family one innocent white lie: that she's been dating her boss. Unfortunately, her boss discovers her lie, and insists on posing as her boyfriend to escort her to the wedding.

Playboy billionaire Dane Prescott always has a new heiress on his arm, but he can't get his assistant Allyson out of his head. He's fought his attraction to her, until he gets caught up in her scheme of a fake relationship.

One passionate weekend with the boss has Allyson Smith questioning everything she believes in. Falling for a wealthy playboy like Dane is against the rules, but if she's just faking it what's the harm?

USA Today Bestselling Author, Lexy Timms, delivers a beautiful tale about a young man who finds love in the least expected place.

Bryan McBride is a disappointment to his parents. Doesn't matter he's a successful architect and that in his spare time he builds homes for the homeless. His tattoos disrespect his family name, his business partner is too blue collar, too surfer, and Bryan's brother—who the family never talks about—died from a drug overdose.

Bryan's passion for art is rekindled when Hailey Ryan comes into town to open a gallery. Without funds to pay for the construction of the gallery, Bryan offers to work in exchange for some of her artwork.

He's caught off guard by the strong attraction he has to her. It's the perfect distraction from the issues in his life he wants to avoid. Except secrets have a way of revealing themselves.

As they begin a passionate love affair, a secret Hailey is keeping threatens to ruin their relationship and possibly their lives.

Capturing Her Beauty

Kayla Reid has always been into fashion and everything to do with it. Growing up wasn't easy for her. A bigger girl trying to squeeze into the fashion world is like trying to suck an entire gelatin mold through a straw; possible, but difficult.

She found herself an open door as a designer and jumped right in. Her designs always made the models smile. The colors, the fabrics, the styles. Never once did she dream of being on the other side of the lens. She got to watch her clothing strut around on others and that was good enough.

But who says you can't have a little fun when you're off the clock?

Sometimes trying on the latest fashions is just as good as making them. Kayla's hours in front of the mirror were a guilty pleasure.

A chance meeting with one of the company photographers may turn into more than just an impromptu photo shoot.

HOT N' HANDSOME, RICH & Single... how far are you willing to go?

Meet Alex Reid, CEO of Reid Enterprise. Billionaire extra ordinaire, chiseled to perfection, panty-melter and currently single.

Learn about Alex Reid before he began Managing the Bosses. Alex Reid sits down for an interview with R&S.

His life style is like his handsome looks: hard, fast, breath-taking and out to play ball. He's risky, charming and determined.

How close to the edge is Alex willing to go? Will he stop at nothing to get what he wants?

Alex Reid is book 1 in the R&S Rich and Single Series. Fall in love with these hot and steamy men; all single, successful, and searching for love.

BOOK ONE IS FREE!

Sometimes the heart needs a different kind of saving... find out if Charity Thompson will find a way of saving forever in this hospital setting Best-Selling Romance by Lexy Timms

Charity Thompson wants to save the world, one hospital at a time. Instead of finishing med school to become a doctor, she chooses a different path and raises money for hospitals – new wings, equipment, whatever they need. Except there is one hospital she would be happy to never set foot in again—her fathers. So of course he hires her to create a gala for his sixty-fifth birthday. Charity can't say no. Now she is working in the one place she doesn't want to be. Except she's attracted to Dr. Elijah Bennet, the handsome playboy chief.

Will she ever prove to her father that's she's more than a med school dropout? Or will her attraction to Elijah keep her from repairing the one thing she desperately wants to fix?

Heart of the Battle Series

In a world plagued with darkness, she would be his salvation.

No one gave Erik a choice as to whether he would fight or not. Duty to the crown belonged to him, his father's legacy remaining beyond the grave.

Taken by the beauty of the countryside surrounding her, Linzi would do anything to protect her father's land. Britain is under attack and Scotland is next. At a time she should be focused on suitors, the men of her country have gone to war and she's left to stand alone.

Love will become available, but will passion at the touch of the enemy unravel her strong hold first?

The Recruiting Trip

Aspiring college athlete Aileen Nessa is finding the recruiting process beyond daunting. Being ranked #10 in the world for the 100m hurdles at the age of eighteen is not a fluke, even though she believes that one race, where everything clinked magically together, might be. American universities don't seem to think so. Letters are pouring in from all over the country.

As she faces the challenge of differentiating between a college's genuine commitment to her or just empty promises from talent-seeking coaches, Aileen heads to the University of Gatica, a Division One school, on a recruiting trip. Her best friend dares who to go just to see the cute guys on the school's brochure.

The university's athletic program boasts one of the top hurdlers in the country. Tyler Jensen is the school's NCAA champion in the hurdles and Jim Thorpe recipient for top defensive back in football. His incredible blue-green eyes, confident smile and rock hard six pack abs mess with Aileen's concentration.

His offer to take her under his wing, should she choose to come to Gatica, is a temping proposition that has her wondering if she might be with an angel or making a deal with the devil himself.

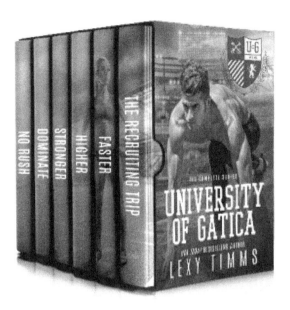

THE ONE YOU CAN'T FORGET

Emily Rose Dougherty is a good Catholic girl from mythical Walkerville, CT. She had somehow managed to get herself into a heap trouble with the law, all because an ex-boyfriend has decided to make things difficult.

Luke "Spade" Wade owns a Motorcycle repair shop and is the Road Captain for Hades' Spawn MC. He's shocked when he reads in the paper that his old high school flame has been arrested. She's always been the one he couldn't forget.

Will destiny let them find each other again? Or what happens in the past, best left for the history books?

Don't miss out!

Click the button below and you can sign up to receive emails whenever Lexy Timms publishes a new book. There's no charge and no obligation.

https://books2read.com/r/B-A-NNL-XOSS

Connecting independent readers to independent writers.

Did you love *Jungle Blaze*? Then you should read *Building Billions - Part 1* by Lexy Timms!

By USA Today Bestselling Author, Lexy Timms.

One night love affair

It was only supposed to be one night. Ashley's just a low step on the ladder of her company's success. The company party was always a big to-do. Jimmy Sheldon, the CEO and found of Big Steps always made sure his employees had a good time. He should, he worked them hard, expected more than they thought they could give, but he always rewarded their efforts. It's what made him a great boss and the owner of a million-dollar company. He knew how to make things work.

And boy, did he.

A few too many cosmo's and Ashley hit the dance floor. She forgot how much fun it was to dance. After a few songs, her years of competitive dance routines came back to her and she had everyone trying to move like her. Even boss-man Jimmy. And he had some decent dance moves himself.

From the dance floor to the hotel room, Ashley swore they'd both forget what happened in the morning and go back to their steps on the ladder.

Except, no one ever forgets a hit song...

Building Billions:

Part 1

Part 2

Part 3

Also by Lexy Timms

A Chance at Forever Series
Forever Perfect
Forever Desired
Forever Together

BBW Romance Series
Capturing Her Beauty
Pursuing Her Dreams
Tracing Her Curves

Beating the Biker Series
Making Her His
Making the Break
Making of Them

Billionaire Holiday Romance Series
Driving Home for Christmas
The Valentine Getaway

Cruising Love

Billionaire in Disguise Series
Facade
Illusion
Charade

Billionaire Secrets Series
The Secret
Freedom
Courage
Trust
Impulse

Building Billions
Building Billions - Part 1
Building Billions - Part 2
Building Billions - Part 3

Conquering Warrior Series
Ruthless

Diamond in the Rough Anthology
Billionaire Rock

Billionaire Rock - part 2

Dominating PA Series
Her Personal Assistant - Part 1
Her Personal Assistant Box Set

Fake Billionaire Series
Faking It
Temporary CEO
Caught in the Act
Never Tell A Lie
Fake Christmas

Firehouse Romance Series
Caught in Flames
Burning With Desire
Craving the Heat
Firehouse Romance Complete Collection

Fortune Riders MC Series
Billionaire Biker
Billionaire Ransom
Billionaire Misery

Fragile Series
Fragile Touch
Fragile Kiss
Fragile Love

Hades' Spawn Motorcycle Club
One You Can't Forget
One That Got Away
One That Came Back
One You Never Leave
One Christmas Night
Hades' Spawn MC Complete Series

Hard Rocked Series
Rhyme

Heart of Stone Series
The Protector
The Guardian
The Warrior

Heart of the Battle Series
Celtic Viking
Celtic Rune

Celtic Mann
Heart of the Battle Series Box Set

Heistdom Series
Master Thief

Just About Series
About Love
About Truth
About Forever

Justice Series
Seeking Justice
Finding Justice
Chasing Justice
Pursuing Justice
Justice - Complete Series

Love You Series
Love Life
Need Love
My Love

Managing the Bosses Series

The Boss
The Boss Too
Who's the Boss Now
Love the Boss
I Do the Boss
Wife to the Boss
Employed by the Boss
Brother to the Boss
Senior Advisor to the Boss
Forever the Boss
Christmas With the Boss
Gift for the Boss - Novella 3.5

Model Mayhem Series
Shameless

Moment in Time
Highlander's Bride
Victorian Bride
Modern Day Bride
A Royal Bride
Forever the Bride

Outside the Octagon
Submit

Reverse Harem Series
Primals
Archaic
Unitary

RIP Series
Track the Ripper
Hunt the Ripper
Pursue the Ripper

R&S Rich and Single Series
Alex Reid
Parker

Saving Forever
Saving Forever - Part 1
Saving Forever - Part 2
Saving Forever - Part 3
Saving Forever - Part 4
Saving Forever - Part 5
Saving Forever - Part 6
Saving Forever Part 7
Saving Forever - Part 8
Saving Forever Boxset Books #1-3

Shifting Desires Series
Jungle Heat
Jungle Blaze
Jungle Fever

Southern Romance Series
Little Love Affair
Siege of the Heart
Freedom Forever
Soldier's Fortune

Tattooist Series
Confession of a Tattooist
Surrender of a Tattooist
Heart of a Tattooist
Hopes & Dreams of a Tattooist

Tennessee Romance
Whisky Lullaby
Whisky Melody
Whisky Harmony

The Bad Boy Alpha Club
Battle Lines - Part 1

Battle Lines

The Brush Of Love Series
Every Night
Every Day
Every Time
Every Way
Every Touch

The Debt
The Debt: Part 1 - Damn Horse
The Debt: Complete Collection

The University of Gatica Series
The Recruiting Trip
Faster
Higher
Stronger
Dominate
No Rush
University of Gatica - The Complete Series

T.N.T. Series
Troubled Nate Thomas - Part 1
Troubled Nate Thomas - Part 2
Troubled Nate Thomas - Part 3

Undercover Series
Perfect For Me
Perfect For You
Perfect For Us

Unknown Identity Series
Unknown
Unpublished
Unexposed
Unsure
Unwritten
Unknown Identity Box Set: Books #1-3

Unlucky Series
Unlucky in Love
UnWanted
UnLoved Forever

Wet & Wild Series
Savage Love
Secure Love
Stormy Love

Standalone

Wash
Loving Charity
Summer Lovin'
Love & College
Billionaire Heart
First Love
Frisky and Fun Romance Box Collection
Managing the Bosses Box Set #1-3